VICIOUS CAROUSEL

Suncoast Society

Tymber Dalton

SIREN SENSATIONS

Siren Publishing, Inc.
www.SirenPublishing.com

A SIREN PUBLISHING BOOK
IMPRINT: Siren Sensations

VICIOUS CAROUSEL
Copyright © 2015 by Tymber Dalton

ISBN: 978-1-63259-936-0

First Printing: October 2015

Cover design by Harris Channing
All art and logo copyright © 2015 by Siren Publishing, Inc.

ALL RIGHTS RESERVED: This literary work may not be reproduced or transmitted in any form or by any means, including electronic or photographic reproduction, in whole or in part, without express written permission.

All characters and events in this book are fictitious. Any resemblance to actual persons living or dead is strictly coincidental.

Printed in the U.S.A.

PUBLISHER
Siren Publishing, Inc.
www.SirenPublishing.com

DEDICATION

For Mr. B.

AUTHOR'S NOTE

This book picks up immediately where *Friends Like These* ends and overlaps slightly with the events in that book. While all the books in the Suncoast Society series are standalone works which may be read independently of each other, the recommended reading order to avoid spoilers is as follows:

1. *Safe Harbor*
2. *Cardinal's Rule*
3. *Domme by Default*
4. *The Reluctant Dom*
5. *The Denim Dom*
6. *Pinch Me*
7. *Broken Toy*
8. *A Clean Sweep*
9. *A Roll of the Dice*
10. *His Canvas*
11. *A Lovely Shade of Ouch*
12. *Crafty Bastards*
13. *A Merry Little Kinkmas*
14. *Sapiosexual*
15. *A Very Kinky Valentine's Day*
16. *Things Made Right*
17. *Click*
18. *Spank or Treat*
19. *A Turn of the Screwed*
20. *Chains*
21. *Kinko de Mayo*
22. *Broken Arrow*
23. *Out of the Spotlight*
24. *Friends Like These*
25. *Vicious Carousel*

Many of the characters in this book appear in previous books in the Suncoast Society series. All titles available from Siren-BookStrand.

VICIOUS CAROUSEL

Suncoast Society

TYMBER DALTON
Copyright © 2015

Chapter One

I am a cliché. Worse, I'm a cliché of a cliché.

She'd known all the "right" things to do, and yet still, she'd found herself slap in the middle of her worst nightmare, the situation everyone had warned her not to let herself get into.

A situation she never thought she'd be in, because here she thought she was different.

Special.

Smarter.

Elizabeth Lambert, known as Betsy to her friends, cowered on the far end of the sofa, sitting with her legs drawn up under her as her boyfriend, Jack, stormed around their duplex apartment. She knew the neighbors next door weren't home, and so did Jack.

Meaning he could ramp up the abuse full-bore without worrying about someone calling the cops on him.

Tonight, Jack was supposed to go work his part-time job as a bouncer at a friend's bar in Bradenton. On most weekdays and every other Saturday, he turned wrenches at a Chevy dealership in Sarasota.

She suspected there was more going on at the bar besides drinking, but she didn't ask.

There were a lot of things she didn't ask anymore, things she should have asked a long time ago, before she'd gotten herself into this position. Eight months ago, she'd had a job as a secretary at a real estate office, a car, a small one-bedroom apartment of her own, and friends.

Now…she just had Jack, and what few things he'd allowed her to keep.

She didn't even have her dignity.

Worse, she wasn't sure exactly how she'd ended up here.

What had happened to the laughing, smiling, charming man who'd swept her off her feet? Who'd said all the right things? Who'd made her feel loved and special?

Yes, she'd only been in the local kinky community a few months when she'd met Jack. He'd just moved down from Michigan, said he wanted to retire in a couple of years, so he'd arranged a transfer from a dealership near Detroit. He was divorced for over twenty years, no kids.

And this Detroit Dom, who seemed to have his act together, who seemed to be able to read her mind about what she wanted and needed, had soon collared her and become her Michigan Master.

The duplex apartment, he'd told her, was temporary. He'd needed a place to stay when he first moved down here, and wanted something economical while he looked for a house. He was waiting for his house in Detroit to sell.

Seemed logical.

So what if it wasn't in the best part of town? It wasn't a crackhouse.

He didn't want any slave of his working, so he'd ordered her to quit.

Since she wouldn't be working, she wouldn't need a car. She could save the expenses by not having one.

When she'd sold it, he'd put the money in his bank account.

She would, of course, live with him. Her apartment lease was due anyway, so he moved her in with him. But he had his own stuff and didn't need hers.

Before she realized it, she was under his thumb, under his control.

And then…

Once he had her trapped, the nice guy she'd fallen in love with disappeared, replaced by a snarling, vicious man she didn't recognize. During one long, lonely day at home, with no access to the Internet because he wouldn't give her the password to the laptop computer that had been hers before he'd confiscated it, and no phone, she was cleaning and came across papers he'd hidden in a suitcase in his closet.

The house in Detroit he'd kept saying he was having trouble selling because of the depressed market there wasn't for sale.

It'd been foreclosed on. Right about the time he'd moved to Florida.

When she'd angrily confronted him about it, that was when the real beatings started.

Followed by the revelation that he'd taken pictures of her while she was blindfolded during some of their private play, and if she didn't toe the line he set for her, exactly the way he set it, her parents would get an earful as well as an eyeful about what their daughter had been up to.

Not that it had stopped him from doing that anyway.

Her parents had disowned her when he told them she was his collared slave.

He'd completely cut her off from everyone and everything.

He owned her, and wouldn't let her go until he was ready. Not that she *could* go anywhere, without a car. Or afford to go anywhere, without a job.

So she sucked it up and tried to figure out a way to get free, except it only got worse.

And then he came home one night a month ago with the chain. Long enough for her to make it all around the apartment, and to the bathroom, but not out the door.

Padlocked tightly around her right ankle when he wasn't home, and securely bolted into the base of the hall wall.

Two weeks earlier, when he'd taken her to the club and marched her around, she'd managed to get permission to use the bathroom. There Loren had slipped a small, pink sticky note to her under the bathroom stall door.

On it, her cell phone number, and Tilly's.

"*Call* us. Day or night. We'll come get you," Loren had whispered before quickly leaving the bathroom.

Betsy had committed the numbers to memory before tucking the note inside the cup of her bra where the push-up pad went.

Right now, she sat cowered at one end of the couch, with her legs tucked under her because she was sitting on the chain, finally free of it. Today, she'd decided she was going to run, with only the clothes on her back, if necessary, and make her escape. She thought she'd have it done and be gone before he returned home, but it had taken her longer to finally work up the nerve to claw it off.

Today, she'd scraped her ankle bloody in the process, but she'd made it, freed herself from the damn chain.

Then, he'd surprised her, came home early, enraged that his manager at work was giving him hassles. She'd sat on the end of the chain, hiding what she'd done.

Unfortunately, she'd had to sit there while he'd pounded her with his fists, unable to defend herself as he took his frustrations out on her.

When he finally finished hitting her, he left her there while he headed for the shower. Then he'd emerged from the shower, took another swipe at her, and left for his other job.

She knew in her heart if she was still there when he got back, he'd do worse to her.

She stayed where she was, perched motionless on the couch, long after she'd flinched at the sound of the door slamming and the echoes of his car driving off had faded from her mind. She waited, waited.

Waited.

It wouldn't be the first time he'd gone off, and then snuck back to try to "catch" her doing something not allowed.

Finally, when over an hour had passed and her feet had gone numb from sitting like that, she slowly, painfully leaned forward, onto her hands and knees, and flopped onto her side.

Feeling began to flood into her feet and lower legs, painful pins and needles. She started flexing her feet, her toes, until she could finally sit up. The world spun and she had to lie down again. When she felt a wave of exhaustion wash over her, she forced herself back up into a sitting position and dared to put weight on her feet.

A new round of pain shot through her, sending adrenaline coursing through her veins as her heart pounded. Her head hurt, so, so bad.

But she'd done it. Despite the bloody furrows in the flesh of her right ankle, she stood, free of the chain.

Slowly shuffling, and with her head held at an angle to keep from tipping over, she trailed one hand along the wall for balance as she headed for the bedroom. The only thing Jack hadn't taken from her was her purse.

Probably because there wasn't anything of value in it. She had her driver's license—not that she'd been allowed to drive in months—and her Social Security card.

Fortunately for her, she'd had fraud protection put on her accounts because of a skimmer getting her debit card number once at a gas station.

She pretended she didn't know how to take it off, so Jack hadn't been able to open any new credit cards in her name. She'd only had one credit card at the time she'd met him, and before she'd moved in with him, she'd used the refund on her apartment security deposit to pay it off.

Without telling him first, which she hadn't thought she'd needed to at the time, and it had earned her a punishment caning.

At the time, he'd followed it with what had felt like a loving, cuddling session, with him reminding her that, as her Master and Owner, she had to run everything through him first.

She'd been in the wrong, or so he'd convinced her at the time.

Betsy found her rolling carry-on bag under the bed and managed to drag it out, using the bed to climb back to her feet. She grabbed underwear, shorts, jeans, a couple of shirts, and a pair of shoes. Even though she had the phone numbers memorized, she found the bra in her drawer and dug the small piece of paper out of the hiding spot, where she'd kept it hidden, just in case.

After pulling on a pair of jeans and a T-shirt, she managed to get her feet into a pair of sneakers. Then she had to sit on the bed for a moment, because…dizzy.

And…

She didn't know why she was so sleepy. It wasn't even…

Carefully turning, she looked at the clock on the bedside table.

Holy shit.

Somehow, it was now nearly ten o'clock. She didn't know if she'd passed out on the couch earlier or what. That meant Jack had actually been gone nearly six hours already.

But she had to get moving. If she didn't, he would beat her mercilessly for getting out of the chain.

She grabbed her purse and the carryon bag and headed for the front door. After a moment of fumbling, where she was afraid maybe she wouldn't be able to get it unlocked, she pulled it open and stared around, in shock that she was, finally, free.

Well, sort of.

She pulled the door shut behind her and locked it with the only key she had since Jack had controlled her life. Yes, she had a few things inside the apartment, some books and photo albums she wanted, but her life was more important.

Getting out wasn't an option anymore. It was mandatory.

She pointed herself toward a convenience store a few blocks away. She didn't dare knock on anyone's door. Jack had threatened her that if she went for help, to be aware that he'd already bribed several of them that they would call him.

That was more than likely a lie, and she knew it, but she wouldn't risk it. It felt like she didn't know anything anymore. What was real, what was lies Jack had told her.

Nothing made sense anymore.

She had heard all the warnings when she got into the lifestyle. Had seen people do stupid stuff. She thought she was smarter.

She thought she knew better.

She thought she was special. Well, even Jack had told her how special she was, and he was able to smooth over every red flag she thought she spotted with such finesse that she didn't know which way was up.

She thought he was going to take care of her.

She thought she'd found the love of her life after years of failed vanilla relationships.

As she trudged through the darkness, she hoped Tilly and Loren had their phones handy. Because if she couldn't get through to them, she damn sure couldn't go back to the apartment.

And she had nowhere else to go.

When she reached the convenience store, the poor clerk looked like he was going to shit himself. It took her several minutes of begging and pleading for him not to call the cops, and to let her use the phone to call her friends.

After she reached Tilly, she sat in the office and burst into tears at the guy's kindness. He used the first-aid kit to tend to her wounds, and even made her an ice pack.

Now she realized how much trouble she was in. Seriously. She wobbled between feeling nauseated and dizzy and sleepy, plus the way her right eye was trying to swell closed, she knew it had to be bad.

She had deliberately avoided looking at herself in the mirror before she left the apartment, not wanting to see how bad it was, afraid the extent of her injuries would weaken her reserve to leave, make her scared of what worse things Jack might do to her if he caught her. It didn't matter that logic told her the police would arrest him for this. It didn't matter that she knew if she had to she could go to an emergency shelter.

The fear would still be there and slide a knife through what little reserve she'd mustered to leave in the first place.

The guy edged a garbage can closer to her. "You don't look so good. Are you sure I can't call 911 for you?"

"No," she said. "My friends will be here soon. They'll take care of me."

She hoped.

"Who the hell did this to you?"

"Someone I never should have trusted in the first place."

Chapter Two

Kenny Yates and Nolan Becker had retreated to a corner of their friends' kitchen. Around them, a private party of the Suncoast Society was in full swing. After the men's rocky encounter earlier that morning with Kenny's step-father, Kenny had counted on getting some bottom time tonight.

Nine years ago, when Kenny was twenty-five, Dennis had married Kenny's mom, Michelle. Michelle had raised Kenny as a single mom, and as long as she got a pre-nup, Kenny told her he'd support her no matter who she married.

She did, and Kenny had done his best to conceal the fact that he was bi from Dennis. Especially while he was dating Nolan—and then moved in with him six years ago.

While Kenny's mom knew the truth, the three of them had been careful not to let Teapublican Dennis in on it. In fact, Kenny's mom thought the two men were gay, not bi.

This morning, while Kenny and Nolan were over helping remove a tree from Kenny's mom's backyard, Dennis had come home early and surprised them…

…and had witnessed Kenny kissing Nolan.

And fireworks of the bad kind had exploded.

Now Kenny wanted a beating and a fucking and a few minutes of subspace to escape from his brain for a while.

"I was thinking," Nolan said as he glanced around, "that it's starting to quiet down a little. You still in a mood to play tonight?"

While they were both Doms, they considered each other equals, which sort of made them both switches.

They could keep it straight, which was both ironic and all that mattered.

Tilly walked into the kitchen and dumped the remnants from a couple of plastic cups into the sink before tossing the cups. "You guys going to play?"

"We were just talking about that," Nolan said.

Tilly smiled. "I know it sounds pervy, but I like watching you two play. I can tell you're having fun. And, no offense, you're both hot."

Kenny laughed. "You've got two hot guys."

"I know I do. And I enjoy watching them together, too. I'm a perv." She shrugged. "What can I say?"

Leigh emerged from the hall leading to the master bedroom with Tilly's purse in her hand. "Sweetie, I love you, but I'm not going into your purse." She set it on the counter.

Tilly looked confused. "Um, why are you bringing this to me?"

Even Kenny jumped when the sound of evil, maniacal laughter rolled from the purse.

Leigh pointed at it. "*That*. Nearly scared the piddle out of me when I went to go to the bathroom."

Tilly dug into her purse. "It's my unknown caller ringtone." She scowled, then answered it. "Hello?"

* * * *

Nolan already knew, deep in his gut, that whoever it was, it wasn't good news. Especially when Tilly started frantically gesturing for something to write with as she attempted to soothe the caller on the other end of the line.

"Whoa, honey, calm down."

The next few minutes of scrambling were a blur as Tilly got the info and a rescue party was assembled, mostly Doms, but also Gabe, who was an armed FDLE agent. Her husband, Bill, was an armed Charlotte County sheriff's detective.

Which wasn't as helpful, since they were in Sarasota County, but hey, they were armed law enforcement officers.

Betsy had been attacked by her boyfriend, and she'd finally found the nerve to escape the abusive, controlling asshole. Kenny and Nolan were no strangers to standing up for themselves or their friends. But as Nolan drove, over the speed limit and close on the heels of Landry and Cris in the vehicle ahead of them, and with a caravan of their friends following behind them, he wouldn't deny that he hoped they weren't in over their heads this time. Tony and Ross rode in their backseat.

"Sorry we won't get to play," Nolan softly said to Kenny.

"This is more important, dude," he said. "Fucker. I hope we get a chance to take a swing at him ourselves."

"There's going to be a really long line for that," Tony said, a hint of murder darkening his tone.

"And I suspect Tilly will occupy the first quarter of that line all on her own," Ross added.

"That sounds about right," Kenny agreed.

Tilly had been enraged that Landry and Cris forced her to stay behind at the house with everyone else, but the last thing they needed was Tilly getting arrested for assaulting Jack.

Besides, someone had to stay behind to bail them all out of jail.

Just in case.

* * * *

When Nolan pulled into the parking lot at the convenience store and they all piled out of their cars, Gabe had made it inside first, the young store clerk pointing toward the office when Gabe flashed her badge.

By the time Nolan and Kenny made it inside, there was already a wall of their friends between them and the office door, making it impossible for them to see.

But they could hear Betsy's tortured sobs.

Once the group parted a few minutes later, and Nolan got his first good look at Betsy, he thought he was going to be sick. The icepack she held over her right eye didn't completely hide the fact that it looked like it'd be swollen closed in a few hours. Over her left eye she bore an ugly laceration the clerk had apparently tried his best to treat with a first-aid kit, several bandages holding it closed. Ugly bruises covered her face and arms.

They all made way as Gabe, now shadowed by Bill, protectively kept her arm around Betsy's shoulders and slowly escorted her outside. Bill carried a purse and carry-on bag Nolan suspected were Betsy's.

Kenny stopped Bill outside. "What's the plan?"

"We're all going to go to her place. It's just five minutes away. Jack's not home, he went to work. We'll get all her shit out of there and move it to Kel's apartment by Venture. She doesn't have a car anymore because the fucker made her sell it and give him the money."

"She'll be alone there at the apartment," Kenny pointed out.

"We'll take shifts—"

"She can stay with us," Nolan interrupted. Kenny looked pleasantly surprised by that declaration, but nodded in agreement.

"Yeah, we've got a spare bedroom," Kenny said. "Half the people at Venture know about Kel's place, now that he's partners with Derrick. That's probably the first place Jack will look for her when he finds out she's gone and once the cops contact him. She can't stay there alone. Jack doesn't know us except from the club. He won't find her with us."

"She's not working right now," Bill said. "The asshole made her quit her job. She can't pay you anything. She doesn't have anything except what Jack didn't make her get rid of."

"We don't care," Kenny and Nolan said together. Kenny continued. "Look, we live within easy walking distance to that new mall. If she can't get a job there, there's a bus stop a block away. She doesn't need to pay us rent until she's able to. We're doing okay."

Bill stared at the two men for a moment before walking around to where Sully and Gabe were getting Betsy settled in the backseat of Bill's car. He leaned in and spoke to them for a moment.

Nolan had always thought Betsy was cute, but before he could have a discussion with Kenny about maybe seeing if she wanted to play with them, Jack, a newcomer from Michigan nearly twice her age, had scooped her up.

And Tony had revealed on the drive over that he'd found out a few tidbits about the guy.

Like that Jack was no longer welcomed in the Detroit area by any of the lifestyle groups there. He hadn't been arrested, as far as Tony knew, but he had a history of doing this kind of thing to young, vulnerable submissives.

Bill returned. "Okay, Gabe signed off on it, and so did Betsy. Although Betsy's really in no condition to be making decisions right now. I suspect if I'd told her we were taking her to Disney she would have agreed. Gabe says we need to take her to the ER, even though Betsy doesn't want to go. She thinks Betsy might have a concussion. And at that point we *will* have local law enforcement involved whether Betsy wants them involved or not."

Bill let out a resigned sigh. "Let's get her stuff first, and we'll talk her into it. The ER trip."

"Thanks," Nolan said. "I promise, we'll take care of her."

Bill arched an eyebrow at him. "If it wasn't for the fact that I know Tilly likes you two a lot, you realize I'd be suspicious right now, right?"

Ross called for everyone's attention. "Let's move. This won't take long, but we need to get it done quick."

* * * *

Kenny was shocked by the duplex apartment. When Bill had told them she didn't have a lot of belongings, he wasn't kidding. It took them less than fifteen minutes to gather all her stuff—and a few things that likely were Jack's, but they were taking for Betsy anyway—and load it into Kel's truck with plenty of room to spare.

When Betsy nearly collapsed in Gabe's arms, Kenny rushed in to scoop her up.

"That's it," Gabe firmly said. "Next stop, ER."

"I don't have insurance," Betsy said. "Please, I'll be okay."

"No, you won't. You've got a concussion. We're taking you to the ER, and we're going to stay by your side while you file the police report."

"He'll kill me if I do."

"No, he won't," Kenny said. "That's not going to happen, because his ass will be in jail."

Gabe stepped in close and looked up into his eyes. "We'll set up some shifts for the first couple of days so she's not alone while you guys are at work."

He nodded.

Betsy clung to him, trembling in his arms. He knew all too well the cautions about risking his heart on a damsel in distress, but watching her quick decline from a vibrant, lovely woman to a battered shell of a person was enough to awaken the protective instincts in him regardless of who she was.

She was one of their friends. Maybe not as close as some of the others, but she was part of their group, their tribe.

Others were willing to stick their necks out for her. He'd be damned if he wouldn't, too.

Nolan pulled his house key off his key ring and handed it to Tony, who would ride with Kel to go deliver her stuff to the men's house before joining them at the hospital. While Nolan did that, Kenny, Sully, and Gabe got Betsy settled once more in the backseat of Bill and Gabe's car.

Then, the slightly reduced procession headed for the hospital. No, they weren't all needed there.

But they would stand by Betsy's side as long as they felt she needed them.

Bill had driven up to the ER entrance. Nolan dropped Kenny and Ross off there and went to go park. Ross ran inside for a wheelchair while Kenny, Sully, and Gabe helped Betsy out. Bill went to go park while Gabe handled dealing with the ER staff.

Only so many of them could be in the room with Betsy at the same time. The natural choices were Bill and Gabe, both active law enforcement officers. With Tony and Kel still gone, it was Kenny and Nolan, Cris and Landry, Ted Collins, Sully, and Ross left to stand vigil in the waiting room.

And as Kenny and Nolan settled in with the rest of their friends in one corner of the ER's waiting room, Kenny realized something.

He leaned in and said in a low voice, "Everyone else is sort of watching us. All of us."

Sully smiled. "Good. Let them."

That late on a Saturday evening, the ER wasn't exactly packed, but there were probably two dozen others there. The extent of Betsy's injuries, and the fact that she had a suspected concussion, had bumped her to the front of the line.

Probably hadn't hurt that both Bill and Gabe had flashed badges at the desk attendant.

While the seven of them had assembled in one corner of the ER, it was like the other people could tell they were…different.

Fortunately, they'd all just come from a private party, designated a pool party-slash-kinky baby shower for Leigh. They were all dressed in either shorts, or jeans, not a stitch of leather clothing among them.

Still, it was as if they gave off a collective "don't fuck with ours" vibe, and the other people felt it.

Landry looked amused. "They're just jealous they're not as cool as us," he drawled.

Bill appeared in the doorway and called for Ted, who was a licensed counsellor, and waved him in.

"That's my cue," Ted said, hurrying to join him.

"I wondered how long until they got him in there," Sully said.

"Good call, asking him to come," Kenny said.

Sully nodded. "I wish I didn't have to say it, but unfortunately, I've dealt with a lot of victims of domestic abuse while I was on the job."

"Why didn't you let Mac come with you, if you don't mind me asking?" Nolan inquired. The two men had had a rather heated-looking discussion, with Clarisse trying to intervene, before Sully had pulled Master rank and loudly ordered Mac to stay behind.

Sully smirked, but it held no humor. "Mac had a sister."

Kenny wasn't sure where their friend was going with this, but he didn't interrupt.

"Okay?" Nolan said.

Sully leaned forward, elbows propped on his knees, hands clasped together, and dropped his voice so it didn't carry beyond their group. "She's how Mac and I first met," he softly said.

Now everyone was leaning in.

"And?" Nolan asked.

"Her name was Betsy, too."

"I'm still not tracking," Nolan said.

Sully let out a heavy sigh. "You've heard the story about how we first met Clarisse, right? How she showed up on our boat? Looking like she'd been beaten within an inch of her life?"

Nolan nodded.

"I was still on the job when Mac and I met. Mac had been on his way to his sister's house to help her move that afternoon. She was going to leave her husband. When Mac arrived, she didn't answer the door. He broke in and found her nearly dead." Sully looked up, pinning first Nolan, then Kenny, with his intense gaze. "Beaten."

Chills ran through Kenny, standing gooseflesh up all over his body.

"She died a couple of days later," Sully continued. "They had to take her off the machines." Sully's gaze dropped to the scuffed linoleum floor. "Don't get me wrong, Mac loves me and Clarisse. I have no doubts about that. But there is no room in our family for any other partners. This is a very raw area for Mac emotionally, a very sensitive trigger. We didn't expect to fall in love with Clarisse, and I'll never regret how things turned out there."

His gaze fell on Kenny this time, piercing, cold. "I'm going to warn you now, it's easy to get too involved in the wrong ways. Be there for her as her friend first. Try to figure out the line between offering her a shoulder to lean on, and picking up and carrying her burdens for her. Let her figure out her life. She's going to need a feeling of safety and security. In our case, Clarisse was terrified of me at first when she found out I used to be a cop, because her ex who nearly killed her was a cop. Well, worked for the police department. Technically he wasn't an actual law enforcement officer. Still, it took me a long time to gradually build her trust in me."

He pointed first at Kenny, then at Nolan. "Stay strong, but stay focused. Don't mistake kindness on your part for a deeper connection. I have a feeling once Betsy heals up that Eliza and Tilly will just about be shoving her at you two."

The other men nodded at Sully's words, also focused on Nolan and Kenny.

"We've always liked her," Nolan said. "As a friend, at least. I promise, we won't rush things or try to make something happen with her."

"It's going to get really rocky, and really messy," Sully warned. "She might fall for both of you as her rescuers, and it will be up to you two to stay strong and wait for her to truly recover in a healthy way before giving in to any temptations just because it's easy. Understand?"

Kenny and Nolan nodded. "Yeah," Kenny said. "We're not looking for anything but to help her out as a friend right now and keep her safe."

Sully reached out a hand to shake with him. "That's a healthy attitude to have, then." They shook, then Sully shook with Nolan. "I would have volunteered to take her up to Tarpon with us, until I realized it was Betsy. Once I heard that, no. With the same name, it's just too much. She needs to be down here, healing down here. And even worse, you—and us all—are her only support net."

"What about her family?" Nolan asked.

Sully looked grim. "The fucker deliberately outed her to her family. Pictures and everything. He must have really thought she was a special target to go after her the way he did."

Ross, who'd been listening to all of that with his head bowed, finally looked up. "We have a spare room," he said. "And Essie's mom lives across the street from us. I know she'd be willing to let her live with her for a while, if needed. Promise us, if things get weird, or don't work out, you won't keep trying to force it to work. Keep us in the loop with her. If she'll work to get herself back on her feet, we'll all help her as much as we can."

"Okay," Kenny said.

"I know she's not some professional victim," Ross said. "I remember Loren and I talking to her when she first started coming out to events. She's a smart, hardworking woman. She had her own place, a good job, a car—she just picked the wrong guy. She told us she had a string of vanilla boyfriends over the years, but she'd never felt right settling down with any of them, and so she didn't. When we warned her about subfrenzy, she assured us she'd be careful and not let some Dom sweep her off her feet and turn her life upside down."

Ross sadly shook his head. "I believed her, too. I really thought she was someone who would do well. She seemed keenly self-aware of what she'd been missing in her life and what she wanted. I thought Loren was going to pop a gasket when she realized that asshole had slapped a collar on Betsy and started reining her in."

"So what do we do about the guy?" Nolan asked.

For his part, Kenny hoped a private "discussion" with the man would be on the agenda.

Somewhere remote.

With quite a few of them in attendance to lay down the new law to the fucker.

A Sarasota County sheriff's cruiser pulled up outside the ER and parked in a specially marked space near the door. The men watched as a female deputy got out, walked into the ER, and spoke to the desk attendant before she was waved inside.

"I think there's your answer right there," Sully said. "If I'm not mistaken, she's here to talk to Betsy."

Chapter Three

Betsy trembled against Gabe as the other woman stood next to the gurney with her arm protectively draped around Betsy's shoulders. It sucked that when they were helping her fill out paperwork, she didn't even know who to put as her next-of-kin contact. Gabe finally filled in Ed Payne's name and cell number. Betsy knew he'd already been called and would help with the legal end of things, but right now, those were details she couldn't even begin to process.

While the doctor examined Betsy and asked her questions, she tried not to fuzz out, to drift away and tune out the world, the pain.

The shame.

A couple of times, Gabe had to gently touch her arm to bring her focus back to them.

"I think you're right that she has a concussion," the doctor said. "We'll get her into radiology immediately."

"I can't afford it," Betsy tried to protest.

"Doesn't matter," Gabe said. "It's getting done."

"Agent Villalobos, how did you say you were involved in this situation?" the doctor asked.

"She's a personal friend," Gabe said. "Several of us were at another friend's house, at a barbecue, when she called one of us. Unfortunately, we've been suspecting he was abusing her for a while. One of our friends reached out to her a few weeks back and made sure she had our cell numbers."

The doctor looked up from the laptop on a rolling stand, where he was taking notes. "But you said she was in a consensual BDSM relationship?"

This was what Betsy had feared. Not being believed. Being discredited because of that.

Worse, now her friends were at risk of being outed for standing up for her.

Bill spoke up. "It started out as consensual, but the man is an abusive predator. No one knew that when she first met him. He didn't have a record, as far as we knew. But once he started isolating Betsy from her support network, the consensual part of their relationship quickly turned into nonconsensual abuse."

The doctor tapped a few more notes into his computer. "And you know this…how?"

She sensed a change come over Bill. "She's a personal friend of ours. And in our group of friends, we take care of our own. None of us could do anything to help her until she reached out and asked for help. Just like any other victim of domestic violence. So if you think you're going to discount her injuries because of her personal interests, *doctor*, then you'd best get me an administrator here *right* now to speak with about reassigning her to another on-call physician who will focus on her physical care and not her personal life."

The doctor, who didn't even look like he was thirty, swallowed nervously and shoved his glasses back up his nose with one finger. "Sorry. I didn't mean to insinuate anything, detective."

Bill gave him a curt nod. "Good." He glanced at Ted, who sat in the corner with his arms crossed over his chest. "Anything you want to add to what I just said, counsellor?"

"Nope. You said it better than I could." Ted smiled. "And as a licensed mental health counsellor, that *is* my professional opinion."

* * * *

When the deputy arrived to take her initial report, Betsy was relieved to see it was a woman. Bill and Gabe stepped outside with the officer for a moment to talk first, while Ted stood and took Gabe's place by her bed.

"I feel bad Nolan and Kenny are going to be put out by this," she said. "I'm afraid for them."

Ted gently held her hand, patting it comfortingly. "Don't worry. They're Tilly-approved."

He smiled, and she tried to return it despite the pain. They'd put stitches in the cut over her left eye, and everything hurt worse than before, especially the wounds on her foot from the chain.

"I wish I'd listened to her to take more time," she softly said. "She asked me when I told her about it if it was what I really wanted, if I didn't want to wait a little longer. I should have listened to her. I thought it was the smart move because my lease was almost up. I thought it made sense to—"

"Don't even go there," Ted warned her. "It happened, and now it's over. You're safe now."

"He could have killed me and my parents wouldn't have ever known it. Just dumped my body somewhere. None of you would have even known it."

"You're going to need to approach your parents at some point and talk to them."

"I can't. He said they hate me. That they're disgusted by me. He made sure of that the first time I said I wanted to talk to him about breaking up."

"Wait," Ted said. "Did *you* actually talk to your parents?"

"I heard him talking to them on the phone. He'd switched into one of his sweet, loving moods and smoothed things over with me. Convinced me to play. Then he tied me up and gagged me and called them and I had to sit and listen to him telling them about us. And he sent them pictures."

"But you didn't actually hear *their* responses? Did he have them on speakerphone or something?"

"I..." She stared at Ted. "No."

“He *told* you he sent them pictures of you, but did your parents actually say anything?”

“I…” She swallowed, despite the pain. “No,” she softly said, not daring to allow hope to break through.

“Okay,” he said, patting her hand again. “For starters, let’s get you healed up and settled in at Nolan and Kenny’s. I don’t specialize in domestic abuse work, but I know a couple of counsellors who do, who are also kink-friendly. I’ll ask around to see if anyone can fit you in for a couple of sessions.”

Fear filled her. “Can you come with me?”

“I’m your friend. I’ll help you with the initial consult with them, if you want, but I really shouldn’t be part of your treatment plan. If we can’t find someone to help you, yes, I’ll try to work with you as much as I can. But I have a professional line I have to be careful not to cross since you’re also my friend. Understand?”

She nodded.

“As your friend, however, I will volunteer to help you talk to your parents, if you want me to.”

She nodded.

“Where do they live?”

“They moved to Virginia a couple of years ago. My dad works for a defense contractor. They moved their facility from Tampa up there.”

“Not to get your hopes up, but there’s a good chance Jack never even talked to your parents that night. He might have cut you off from them, but that all might have been faked on his end that night.”

“I hope so.” She didn’t dare hope, though. Not really.

Not deep inside her soul.

The deputy returned with Bill and Gabe. Ted resumed his seat in the corner of the room while the deputy took Betsy’s report and more pictures of her injuries to supplement the ones the ER staff had already taken. Before she’d finished, a male detective had arrived, shaking hands with Bill when he spotted him there.

They all once again stepped out into the hall to talk while Ted returned to Betsy's side. "Looks like that's Bill's friend he mentioned."

"Good," she said. "Will they arrest Jack tonight?"

"Probably. There's pretty conclusive evidence. And there's the damn chain." Ted's face went dark, unreadable. "Let me tell you something," he softly said. "If you ever find yourself in trouble again, *ever*, you call any of us. Day or night. We'll get you a cellphone, program everyone's numbers into it, and you keep it on you always. Understand?"

"I can't afford—"

"Stop. We get it. He isolated you from everything and took everything from you to keep you dependent upon him. After you're healed up, we'll work with you on your resume and get you another job somewhere, start getting you back on your feet. Between us, believe me, we can afford a cheap-ass pre-paid cell phone just so we have peace of mind that you are safe."

She wanted to cry, felt like crying, but maybe it was the meds or that she'd already cried what felt like gallons of tears, because she felt empty, barren. "Thank you."

"No worries."

Everyone returned. After another round of questions interrupted by a trip to radiology for an X-ray, she finished her talk with the detective, who'd phoned in a request for a search warrant for the apartment.

Oh, the irony. Technically they didn't need one since she was a resident of the apartment and gave them permission to search it, but out of an abundance of caution to not to do anything to mess up the case, they requested one.

Despite the ER doctors wanting to keep her for observation, Betsy signed herself out against doctor's orders and made sure to give the rest of her friends hugs in the waiting room as Gabe wheeled her out.

Tony and Kel had returned. "We called Ed Payne," Tony said. "He'll be meeting with you in the morning to help you file an emergency restraining order."

"Thank you." Everything felt like a pain-filled, nightmarish blur. "Thank you, everyone. I can't tell you how much I appreciate this."

With a smaller contingent this time, she rode with Bill, Gabe, and Sully back to the apartment, while Kenny and Nolan, the deputy, and the detective followed.

Two more patrol deputies and another detective arrived at the apartment as the first detective was taking pictures of the chain, the dried blood on it, for evidence.

"Search warrant," the newly arrived detective said, holding up one piece of paper. "And bench warrant," he said, holding up the other. "Two officers are already heading toward the bar to pick him up."

"Do I have to be here when you get him?" she asked, terrified to face Jack this soon.

"No," the detective told her. "We'll need you to come in in the morning and answer some more questions, but you don't have to see him right now."

"Thank you," she said.

They got her back in the car. Then, she figured the pain shot she'd received had knocked her out at some point. She awoke to Gabe gently touching her shoulder.

They were parked outside an unfamiliar house, and Bill, Sully, Kenny, and Nolan stood waiting.

"We're here," Gabe said.

"Where?"

"Kenny and Nolan's. Remember? We told you you'll be staying here with them."

"Oh. Okay." She did remember something about that, but everything hurt, and now her right ankle, which before had been sore, felt like it had rusty barbed wrapped around it.

Hell, everything hurt.

Jack. Oh, yeah. Jack happened.

They finally got her out of the car. Gabe and Bill, with Sully close behind, walked her up to the front door where Nolan and Kenny led the way inside and down a hallway.

They flipped the light on in a strange bedroom she'd never seen before, but she recognized her things—what things she'd still had—stored around the room.

"Tony put your stuff in the bathroom across the hall," Nolan said. "That's all yours to use. There's towels and stuff in there, too, when you're ready to take a bath."

Kenny pulled down the covers for her as Gabe and Bill carefully lowered her to the bed. Sully knelt and helped her remove her shoes, a pained hiss escaping her when he did the right one.

"Sorry, honey," he apologized. "Consider that a badge of courage when you're in a better frame of mind. That was a brave thing you did tonight. You have no idea."

"I don't feel very brave," she softly said.

Gabe rooted through her things and found a pair of sweatpants for her to put on instead of jeans, which meant getting her back onto her feet and down to the bed again.

Gabe and Bill helped her lie down, tucked her in, and Kenny left the bedside lamp on for her when she asked for a light to be kept on.

They all bid her good-night and closed the door behind them.

Before she could even roll over, she felt blackness take her.

* * * *

Nolan waited until they reached the living room. "Fucking son of a bitch," he said, his tone murderous. "I will fucking beat the everloving shit out of that bastard if he fucking gets out of jail. I will hunt him down and kill him."

Gabe smiled and put her fingers in her ears. "Lalalala—you'd better let me help—lalalala."

Bill took a deep breath, which escaped him in a sad sigh. "No one's killing him. He'll go through the system and hopefully end up in jail for a while, unless they let him plead out. I know Tony said he didn't think anyone had pressed charges against the guy, but it doesn't mean Jack doesn't have a sheet on him somewhere. If he does, then all the better for this case against him."

Sully looked grave. "You two realize there will likely be some press about this, right? 'Woman kept chained and beaten in BDSM sex dungeon.' I'm sure that will be the gist of the headlines once this makes the blotter and a reporter gets hold of it."

Nolan nodded. "I know. It's okay. Our jobs are secure. We're county employees without morality clauses. We're just her friend. Jack tries to sling dirt at us, it won't stick."

"It's going to get ugly," Sully said. "He'll probably have a public defender—if we're lucky—who will try to talk the asshole into copping a plea deal. But don't be surprised if Jack slings mud like a monkey flings its shit."

"Thank god he was never invited to any of the private parties," Gabe said.

"This is the exact reason why Lucas and Ross carefully cherry-picked the attendance roster tonight," Sully said. "Tony's the only one of us who went on the rescue mission tonight who's extremely vulnerable in this matter."

"What about you two?" Nolan asked Bill and Gabe.

They smiled at each other. "My former boss is a member of Venture," Gabe said.

"And Jack doesn't know who the hell I am or what I do. Either one of us," Bill said. "The story we told tonight was that we were at a friend's house for a barbecue, the call came in, and because we're law enforcement, naturally we volunteered to help."

"But," Sully continued, speaking to Nolan and Kenny, "if you two can't handle what might happen, you need to reach out immediately. You heard Ross. He and Loren can take her in, and they're pretty insulated from anything Jack might try. Doesn't hurt that Ross is an attorney, too, even though he doesn't practice criminal law."

Kenny looked at Nolan. Nolan was pretty sure the grim expression his partner wore mirrored his own. "We've got this," Kenny assured them. "As long as she needs or wants to be here, we've got this."

"Okay." Sully shook with them both again. "I consider that a promise that I'll hold both of you to."

After saying good-night to them, Nolan locked the door behind them before turning to Kenny. "Wow."

Kenny headed for the kitchen. "Wow, indeed. Oh, dammit." He turned. "Our implement bag's still at their house."

Nolan followed him to the kitchen. "If that's the worst thing you can think of right now, you're doing better than I am."

"I'm *not* thinking right now," Kenny said as he rummaged in the fridge and emerged with a bottle of hard apple cider. He held it up to Nolan, who shook his head.

Kenny closed the fridge and popped the cap with a magnetic church key from the front of the fridge. He drained half the bottle in two swallows.

"Do we need to set up some ground rules?" Nolan asked.

Kenny leaned against the counter and slowly nodded. "You're reading my mind again, buddy." His brown gaze focused on Nolan. "I'm thinking hands-off, totally, for the foreseeable future. Friends-only."

Nolan nodded. "Yep." He stepped in close, pressing Kenny back against the counter as he wrapped his arms around his partner's waist. "My thoughts exactly."

"What do we consider the gateway to untabling this topic?" Kenny asked. "Just in case."

"I don't know." He kissed Kenny, enjoying the taste of hard cider on his lips. "I say we don't have one. We watch and wait. She might decide she would rather go to Ross and Loren's, once she's able to think straight. I will honestly be surprised if she wakes up and remembers most of tonight as out of her mind as she was with pain and fear."

"True." Kenny took another swallow from the bottle. Nolan couldn't help that the motion reminded him of how Kenny looked with Nolan's cock between his lips.

"Or," Nolan added, "she might get her act together and get her own place sooner rather than later."

"Also true," Kenny said. "I would like to add if she brings it up, or it becomes a discussion Tilly or Eliza force with her, I'm okay saying she's under our protection without it being anything more. As long as everyone else thinks that's a good idea."

Nolan considered it and nodded. "I'm good with that. It might be what she needs to feel safe."

"I hope this experience doesn't drive her out of the lifestyle altogether." A dark frown clouded Kenny's expression. "I remember when we talked to her when we first met her. How excited she was. How she said she felt like she finally belonged somewhere. That she didn't feel weird or different anymore."

"Yeah," Nolan sadly said. "Me, too. I thought she was adorable." Kenny's attention snapped onto Nolan. "What?" Nolan asked.

Kenny took a moment to answer. "Long-term. *If*," he strongly emphasized, "she is in a healthy place, I'm not against you and me talking about maybe more than just protecting her."

"Long-term," Nolan agreed. "And *only* if, *after* we bounce it off others first, they think it's a good idea."

Kenny rested his head against Nolan's shoulder. "What time is Ed getting here?"

"We're supposed to call him, but he said he wanted to be here by ten."

"Okay. I hope she's awake by then."

"Why do I have a feeling our world just shifted?"

“Because it did.” Kenny kissed him before slipping past him and heading for the kitchen doorway, where he pulled up short. “Oh, dammit.” He turned.

“What?”

“Mom’s coming for dinner tonight.”

“So?”

Kenny pointed down the hall. “*So*? Really?”

“We tell the truth. She’s a friend in trouble. If Dennis comes with her, maybe it’ll make him keep his mouth shut around Betsy.”

“I should cancel dinner.”

“No.” Nolan walked over to him and pulled him in close again. “I don’t want to cancel dinner. I suspect Mom’s going to need to get out of the house, and I’d really be shocked—like buy a lotto ticket shocked—if Dennis came with her. Maybe having Mom here to talk to might help Betsy.”

“You think so?”

“I think it’ll help take Mom’s mind off her troubles.” There was a little hard cider left in the bottom of the bottle. Nolan took it from Kenny and drained it, then put it in the recycling bin under the sink. He returned to Kenny and took his hand. “Sorry you didn’t get your beating and fucking.”

Kenny shrugged. “To be honest? I’m too exhausted and mentally wrung out for either right now. But, hey, bonus, shift in perspective. Having a homophobic douche for a step-dad is no biggie, in the grand scheme of things.”

Nolan chuckled as he led him down the hall toward their bedroom. “That’s putting it into perspective, all right.”

Chapter Four

Betsy startled awake the next morning, her left eye wide, right eye unable to open, fear spiking adrenaline through her system and making her heart jackhammer in her chest.

Fear even overshadowed the disorientation she felt as her one-eyed gaze darted around the room, taking in the unfamiliar surroundings.

This wasn't Jack's bedroom.

This *damn* sure wasn't Jack's bed—and thank god for that, because it was like a thousand times more comfortable.

She sucked in a deep breath and let it out again as her mind slowly began to turn and settle back into place, the events of the previous evening coming back to her. Getting the chain off her foot.

Getting free.

But how free was she, really?

She literally had no money. Worse, now she had a hospital bill she'd have to figure out how to pay. At least with Jack, she wasn't in debt, not that he wouldn't have loved to put her there and even more firmly under his thumb.

She wanted to sit up, but when she tried to lift her head she realized that wasn't going to be possible. Pain, sharp and piercing, slammed through her skull. And that made her wince, which made all her other pains speak up and holler for attention, including the agony in her right ankle. She laid back down again, her eyes squeezed closed, as she prayed for the pain to abate.

Shit.

Breathing hurt. Hell, *thinking* hurt.

After a couple of minutes, she realized she would have to move eventually. She slowly reached out with her left hand and couldn't feel the edge of the bed.

Okay, that means I'm on the right side.

Sure enough, slow and careful exploration with that hand allowed her to discover the edge and showed her how much room she had to work with so she didn't roll her stupid ass right off onto the floor.

Taking a couple of long, slow, deep breaths, she gingerly tried rolling onto her right side. It took every ounce of strength she had not to scream in agony.

Dammit.

Okay, getting up on her own wasn't an option at that time.

Moving slowly, she turned her head toward the left. Outside, light leaked around the edges of the horizontal blinds covering the windows. As she tried slowly moving her head back to the right, she spotted the time on a cable box.

7:27

Okay. I have to get up.

She gave up when a dizzying wave of vertigo accompanying the spike of pain swept over her on her second attempt to lift her head.

Somewhere out in the house, she heard someone moving around and smelled coffee brewing. It made her stomach growl.

Yeah, come to think of it, she hadn't eaten anything since breakfast Saturday morning. She wasn't allowed to eat unless Jack gave her permission. If he came home and found stuff missing from the fridge or cabinets without him okaying it, he would beat her for it. He'd said she needed to lose weight, even though she hadn't thought she was fat.

I hope he's in jail.

Screw that, she hoped he was *under* the fucking jail.

In the cold light of day, as her new reality slowly began to sink in, she realized survival mode was no longer necessary. She *had* survived, despite what she'd stupidly let him do to her.

There had been plenty of hours, alone in the apartment with nothing but basic cable and a few books, where she'd thought about her predicament and how to get out of it. Sure, before the chain, she could have simply packed all her stuff and walked away.

Except she hadn't known who to call for help.

Despite that, she'd just about talked herself into getting away. Maybe there'd been a determination in her demeanor. Maybe the way she'd thrown herself into obeying his every order as quickly and perfectly as possible as a way to pull him off-guard and lull him into a false sense of complacency had backfired on her.

That was when he'd brought home the chain.

And then she was *really* stuck. She no longer had a cell phone. Jack had confiscated her laptop, changing the password and using it as his own. She remembered seeing it gone last night when they returned to the apartment with the detectives, so she guessed it'd been grabbed when everyone got her stuff.

Well, it was pink, so it was an easy thing to think. It was probably there in the room, somewhere, with her other things.

She'd have to ask Tony if he could hack the password for her.

Another noise from out in the kitchen, and she kicked her pride in the ovaries and took a deep breath.

"Hello?" She didn't want to yell *help* and scare the poor guys to death.

At first, she wasn't sure she'd called out loudly enough, but then she heard a soft knock on her door.

"Betsy?" It sounded like Nolan.

"Yes," she said, trying not to break down and cry. "I need help, please."

Nolan opened the door and poked his head through, a look of concern on his face. "What's wrong?" He wore a dark green bathrobe.

Her tears finally broke free. "I can't get up by myself. I'm sorry. I need help. It hurts too much."

He swooped in, her knight in shining terry cloth, and helped her sit up as she bit down on the scream of pain that wanted explode from her.

"Pain?" he asked.

"And dizzy," she said.

"That's probably the concussion. You should have let them admit you last night."

"I can't afford it. Can you please help me into the bathroom?"

"Sure."

He gently helped her swing her legs around and then once again held her, lifting her more than her actually standing under her own power. Slowly, he matched her pace as she shuffled toward the door.

Kenny appeared, wearing nothing but a pair of boxers and looking half asleep, his hair tousled. "Are you all right?"

"No, she's not," Nolan said. "She can barely move. Help me."

Kenny also swooped in, and together, the men got her across the hall and into the bathroom. Shoving modesty aside, she asked them to stay while she got herself onto the toilet with their help and did what she needed to do. At least she could wipe herself. Then they helped her stand, Kenny deftly pulling her pajama pants up before they got her over to the sink.

That was when she made the mistake of lifting her head and looking into the mirror. The sob she let out sounded forged in some deep, toxic swamp, even to her own ears.

Yes, her right eyelid and the surrounding flesh was a dark, purple, swollen mass.

Which explained why it wouldn't open, duh. Over her left eye, a bruise surrounded the laceration where stitches held it closed. Her face looked unrecognizable, even to her. In the mirror she could see the bruises around her neck, along her arms.

"I look like shit," she whispered.

Both men wore grim expressions as they silently nodded.

And her right ankle hurt like a fucking son of a bitch.

She got her hands washed and carefully brushed her teeth, even though that was a horrible act of masochism in and of itself. Somehow, she miraculously still *had* all her teeth.

"Back to bed?" Nolan gently asked when she finished.

She shook her head. "No. Did I hear an attorney was coming by this morning?" Great, more money she didn't have and couldn't afford, but she wouldn't refuse the help.

"Yeah, Ed Payne," Nolan said. "He's a member of the Suncoast Society group. He said he's met you before at munches, but you might not remember him until you see him."

"Okay. I guess I should have a shower." The thought of trying to do that, though, filled her with dread. She really wanted to shave her legs, but that would be impossible. She needed to wash her hair. Hell, she needed to *brush* her hair and didn't think she could even do that.

The men exchanged a dubious glance over her head, which she spotted in the mirror.

She drew in a pained breath. "Look, I'm beyond the bashful stage. I get it, I'm a wreck. I would really appreciate it if you would help me get a shower. I promise I won't freak out over incidental contact."

Nolan shucked his bathrobe. Under it, he wore silk boxers with smiley faces on them.

She couldn't help it. She laughed, even though that fucking hurt like hell. "I'm sorry," she said. "They're adorable."

"I was going to give you my robe to cover up with after your shower," he said.

"Sorry." But she smiled, even though it hurt like unholy *fucking* hell.

After getting her undressed, the men helped her step into the shower. Kenny found her hairbrush in her purse and brought it in. The men worked together, while she stood there with her left arm braced against the shower wall for balance, to brush out her hair without pulling on it too much.

She wanted to break down crying from the tenderness of their actions, but managed to choke her tears back. She didn't want them to think they were hurting her.

She was hurting, but not because of them. She also realized she would have to watch herself, not throw herself into some stupid sort of trap of falling for them because they were the ones here helping her, and misplace her affections for them.

It would be too easy, after the hell she'd been through, to fall for someone…kind.

Non-assholish.

Even a guy who was slightly a jerk, but not abusive.

Nope. Not again. Yes, she knew what she wanted and needed, but she obviously wasn't any better at picking out kinky partners than she had been at picking out vanilla ones.

For now, she was off the market. She would get her shit together, get her life together, figure out how to become independent again, and then, *maybe*, she'd think about playing.

She wouldn't even date. Screw that. She could play with someone and get orgasms, never even leave the goddamned club with them, say good night to them, and go home, safely, alone, and without worrying about getting punched because she ate three too many pieces of macaroni.

If someone wanted a relationship with her, they would have to fucking bend over backward like the goddamned Rubber Man to prove they weren't faking it until she decided to submit to them and let them have control over her.

Even then, she wasn't sure, after this, if she ever could open herself up to that kind of relationship again. It was what she desperately wanted, even needed, but not now…

Maybe never again.

The death of that possibility hurt almost as much as her physical injuries.

"I'm sorry," she said as they finished brushing out her unruly brown hair.

Jack had ordered her to grow it long. She preferred keeping it around shoulder length, just long enough to pull back if she had to, but with its natural curliness, at that length it was easy to wear loose and natural if she used product in it to keep it from frizzing out.

Not that he'd let her buy anything other than the cheapest shampoo possible.

"Why are you apologizing?" Nolan asked.

"Because I know this is a pain in the ass," she said. "And I appreciate the help."

Kenny picked up the bottle of shampoo and looked at it. "Whoa. No offense, this is what you like using?"

"No. I hate it It's all he'd let me buy. It was the cheapest stuff."

"Hold on." She heard him mutter something under his breath as he turned and left the bathroom. When he returned a moment later, he carried a bottle of shampoo and one of conditioner. "Sorry they're not perfect for your hair type, but it's better than that shit."

They took the handheld showerhead down, started the water, and got it warmed up. Working together, the two men shampooed her hair and then applied the conditioner, letting it sit while one of them soaped up a washcloth and gently started working on her legs and arms.

She hissed with pain when the cloth touched her right ankle.

"Sorry," Kenny said. "It's rough." The doctor had left it unbandaged and told her to keep an eye on it, keep it clean, and to put antibiotic ointment on it if it looked like it might be getting irritated, but that the best thing for it would be to heal without a bandage. The links of the chain had dug into her flesh as she'd first tried soap and water, and then a little olive oil, to slide it off over her skin.

"It's okay," she said. "It needs to be washed off."

It had been brute force and desperation that finally did the trick, hence why she'd been sitting on the couch to do it, and hadn't moved yet when Jack had arrived home early.

But there'd been rough points on some of the links that dug in deeper than others. They gave her a tetanus booster at the hospital last night, just in case, because she couldn't remember the last time she'd had one.

"Can I ask a dumb question?" Nolan said.

"Yeah."

"Why the chain? How long had that shit been going on?"

"Only a couple of weeks," she admitted. "I think he did it because he realized I was getting close to leaving."

"Ah," Kenny said. "Trying to rein you in even more, huh?"

"Yeah."

As they bathed her, she softly told them the full story, somehow managing not to cry her way through it. When she finished, both men remained silent.

"Well?" she asked.

Nolan let out something that sounded like a disgusted grunt. "I'm sorry this happened to you. You're a good person. He preyed on your trust."

"I'm a dumbass, is what I am," she said. "I ignored red flags. Well, in my defense, he was good at hiding the red flags at first. I let him sweet-talk me. Had I held my ground longer, he probably would have lost interest in me and moved on to someone else. The more he hooked me in, the more I was hooked, until I didn't realize that he was just reeling me in and dangling me on the end of his line like a trophy bass. I accept I was stupid."

"Not all men are like that," Nolan said.

"I know. But for now, I plan on getting my life back together. The last thing I need right now is a relationship."

* * * *

Kenny wasn't sure, but he thought Nolan also breathed a sigh of relief at Betsy's statement. If she stuck to her guns, she had a good chance of pulling herself out of this.

He handed her the washcloth to finish cleaning between her legs and washing her breasts. Helpful or not, he preferred to avoid those areas right now if she was capable of doing it. Not that he didn't find her attractive, because he did, but he also wanted to try to keep a healthy boundary between them if possible.

After they rinsed the soap off her, Kenny draped a towel around her and gently patted her dry while she stood there. Her right side was turned toward him, and her swollen eye nearly made him sick to look at. The level of violence she'd endured was horrific.

After getting her out of the shower, Nolan draped his robe around her and they walked her back into the bedroom.

"I packed some stuff in that overnight bag of mine," she said. "Just dig something out of there for now, please."

"Okay." Kenny found it and opened it, spreading clothes out on the bed. She pointed to a long jersey-knit skirt, a short-sleeved tunic, and a pair of underwear.

"I'm not even going to try for a bra," she said. "I might be a masochist, but that's pushing it, even for me."

They helped her get dressed and then walked her out to the living room, where they eased her down onto the couch and handed her the remote control.

"Coffee?" Nolan asked.

"Please. I feel stupid asking this, but do you have a cup with a straw, and could you put a couple of ice cubes in it to cool it down? I don't think I could handle it all the way hot right now, and cold wouldn't be good, either."

"Of course. Milk and sugar?"

"Lots of both, please."

Kenny showed her how the remote worked while Nolan fixed her coffee. "We'll call Ed, grab our showers, and then make you something to eat."

"I'm not sure what I can eat," she said.

"Scrambled eggs? Oatmeal?"

She slowly nodded. "Eggs sounds good," she sadly said. "Thank you."

"What's wrong?" Kenny asked her. "I mean, besides the obvious."

Her sad, lopsided smile twisted his heart. "Do you know the last time I had eggs for breakfast?"

He shook his head.

"Do you know what my required breakfast has been the past couple of months?"

"What?"

"A quarter cup of Cheerios, dry, an apple or a banana, and two cups of water."

He frowned. "What?"

"I was trying to please him. At first, I thought okay, yeah, maybe I could stand to lose a couple of pounds." She sadly shook her head. "It wasn't just about that. I realized it was about control. His control of me. Down to the ounce."

"How long had you been planning to leave?"

"Before the damn chain? Over a month. I decided to be the perfect slave, do everything he said, exactly as he said, no matter what. I was trying to make him think I was working my ass off—literally—to please him."

Her left eye stared down at her lap. "I think that's why he bought the chain. Because he was either suspecting I was up to something, or he was further testing me. That's why I let him put it on me at first. I thought okay, if I fight this, he'll know. So I acted like I was happy to obey. *That* was a mistake, and I didn't realize how bad a mistake it was. The abuse ramped up from there."

"I thought Ross said you were at the club a few weeks ago? That Loren slipped you phone numbers?"

"I was. Jack would beat me where the bruises wouldn't show, or where they'd look like they belonged. There were also face slaps, things like that, but nothing to leave a mark, usually. But after that night at the club, it's like he knew, and things went downhill fast. Part of me wonders if it was a test to see if I'd still be there when he got home later. If so, if he followed his normal pattern, he likely would have apologized, been all sweet and nice, treated me like a princess until I healed up."

"And then he'd do it again."

She reached up and touched her nose.

"Shit."

"I've learned my lesson, don't worry. And thank you for opening your home to me. I promise I'll try to get out of your way as soon as I can, and I'll pull my weight while I'm here." She harshly laughed. "Well, once I can walk on my own. I'll do chores and stuff until I can afford to pay rent. And even after, of course."

He touched her shoulder. "You're welcomed to stay here as long as you need, and stop worrying about money. Please don't rush to get out of here on our account. You focus first on healing, then the rest will follow."

"Thank you."

Nolan brought her coffee with a straw, a glass of water with a straw, and three ibuprofen. She swallowed the ibuprofen first with the water, then sipped the coffee through the straw.

"It's perfect, thanks."

They left her sitting there and retreated to their bedroom to call Ed.

Chapter Five

The men quickly showered and dressed and made breakfast for themselves and Betsy. They were ready to go when Ed arrived. He drove, Nolan riding in the backseat with Betsy. Everything hurt, but she wanted this done, and as soon as possible.

At the building where the sheriff's detective was stationed, a receptionist made them wait in the lobby until the detective came out to greet them. Ed took the lead, introducing everyone.

"Ms. Lambert," the detective said, "thank you for coming back in this morning."

"Did you arrest him?" Ed asked.

"He's in jail right now. He'll be arraigned later today."

"Will he make bail?"

"That depends on the judge. The case is…complicated."

"Complicated how?" Betsy asked, her stomach churning. She suspected she knew exactly what "complications" would get thrown in her face.

"Let's go talk in private."

He led them to a conference room and had them wait there while he grabbed his laptop and some files.

"Turns out that Mr. John Bourke, aka Jack, has been in trouble with the law before, about twenty years ago," the detective said.

Her stomach fell. "He was?"

"He had four years' probation for assault on one Mrs. Jill Bourke. They were in the middle of a divorce at the time."

"That's all?" Ed asked. "No outstanding or recent cases?"

"That's where it gets interesting. He was the subject of two calls for service in Detroit, for what sounded like domestic disturbances, but no charges were ever filed in those cases. Those happened just a couple of months before he moved down here. There was another complaint filed against him six months before those, but the witness withdrew her complaint and refused to testify. Prosecutors had to drop the case due to lack of evidence."

"The son of a bitch is going to try to use BDSM as a defense," she said. "He's going to threaten to release pictures he took of me to try to get me to recant."

Then again, she'd heard Tony say something about finding a camera last night. Wouldn't surprise her if that had also ended up with her stuff.

She could only hope it had.

"He is claiming the two of you had a consensual relationship," the detective said. "That you agreed to the chain."

"I didn't agree to it. I was scared to refuse it. I was ordered to wear it. So no, I didn't fight him, but the fact that I clawed it off my leg yesterday, along with a good chunk of my own skin, should be proof that I wasn't willingly wearing it."

The detective walked her through her story again, checking his notes as he went. Now, without fear pressed against her spine like a straight razor, she was able to take her time, be reasonably cogent, remember details she might have forgotten to tell them the night before.

There was a knock on the door and a woman stuck her head in. "Barbara Stallings, state attorney's office."

The detective waved her in. "Perfect timing."

Betsy let Ed and the detective get the attorney up to speed. Then Stallings looked from Nolan to Kenny. "And you two gentlemen are?"

"Her friends," they said together. "And," Nolan added, "she's staying with us for now."

"I'm filing for the TRO after we're done here," Ed told Stallings. "Mr. Bourke doesn't have any idea where Mr. Becker and Mr. Yates live, so she's safe with them."

The government's attorney sat back and eyed them all. "Between you and me and the fencepost," she said, "I don't care what people do in their bedrooms. You're all 'friends in common,' as they say, aren't you?"

Ed glanced at the two men before focusing on the attorney again. "We all have a lot of friends in common, yes. It was other friends who vouched for these two men as a safe place for her to stay while she tries to get her life back together. If she goes to a shelter, she'll only be there for a short while anyway. Her friends wanted to step in to help her get her life back in order. There's nothing wrong with that."

"No, there's not. I just want to know what I'm dealing with. I'm no stranger to alternative lifestyle dynamics. I've seen a lot, and I don't judge. I can see this is obviously not a consensual level of injury here. But the ankle chain is going to come into play, that she wore it for several weeks before all of this happened."

"He didn't even know I'd taken it off when he beat me," Betsy said. "I was sitting on it. I heard him drive up and hid it under me."

Stallings leaned forward, arms crossed in front of her and resting on the table. "Miss Lambert, if you had the chain off, why didn't you run when he started beating you?"

"I couldn't," she said. "He would have seen I had gotten free. I was afraid he'd catch me and hurt me worse. I didn't know he was going to attack me the way he did. And, hello, I was naked at the time, so it would have been difficult getting away without clothes."

Stallings nodded. "Okay. That makes sense. Just remember, if this goes to trial, his attorney will be asking you questions like that. I will not tell a witness what to say, but I'm sure Mr. Payne here will be able to help you understand the kind of character assassination you'll be subjected to if you're forced to testify against Mr. Bourke. I'm going to do my best to get him to plead out to something reasonable, but I can't promise that will happen."

"Bail?" Ed asked.

"Felonious assault, false imprisonment, battery, extortion—I've got a grocery list of charges I'm going toss at him when he's arraigned. Not all of them will stick all the way through to trial, especially if he pleads out, but the more I throw at him, along with his previous conviction for assault, I'm going to ask for two-fifty."

"But he won't get that," Ed said.

"Probably not. Probably lucky if they give him one hundred thousand. But he might not be able to make bail. If so, then lucky us, he can sit there and rot in a cell while I dangle a deal in front of an overworked and underpaid PD who doesn't want to defend an abuser in the first place. This isn't a 'he-said, she-said' kind of situation with no visible wounds, obviously."

Once they finished there, Ed drove them to another building where Betsy had to speak to a judge in chambers before Ed filed paperwork.

Then, they headed back to Kenny and Nolan's house. Before Ed left, he said, "I'll follow the arraignment and let you know what happens. Is there anything else at the apartment you need to get?"

She shook her head. "No."

"You mentioned pictures. Do you think he has any memory cards or anything?"

Nolan nodded. "There was a camera, Tony said. Hold on." He went to what was now her bedroom and they heard him digging around. A few minutes later, he returned with a computer bag—what had been her computer bag, holding what had been her computer—and a camera case.

The men searched through them. On the camera, dozens of pictures, including ones of her during play and after "punishments." And several other memory cards.

“I don’t know if he had any other memory cards besides those,” she said.

“What about the computer?” Ed said.

“It was mine, but he took it and changed the password. Do you think Tony can fix it?”

“I’ll take it to him and see,” Ed told her. “Was the camera yours, too?”

She nodded.

“Okay, good. Then they’re your property. Do I have your permission to go through them, and the computer, for evidence?”

“Yeah. Of course.”

“Good. I’ll call the guys later and let you know what’s going on.”

“Thank you, Ed. I’ll find a way to pay you back for all your trouble.”

“Maybe,” he said. “If not, don’t worry about it. I help my friends, and you’re one of my friends. We take care of our own, you know.”

Once he was gone, the men got her settled on the couch. “Can we get you anything to eat or drink?” Kenny asked.

“No, I just need to rest, I think. Is it okay if I turn the TV on and take a nap out here? I don’t want to be alone in my room right now. I’ve spent enough time alone the past several months.”

“Sure,” Nolan said. “You get comfy. I’ll go get you some pillows.”

* * * *

Kenny followed him to her room. “I’ll call Mom and cancel,” he whispered.

“Don’t you dare,” Nolan whispered back.

“What if Dennis comes?”

“So? We’re not changing our lives for him. Mom will understand us helping her.”

Kenny sighed. "I should go get her some stuff. She barely has anything."

"Like what?"

"Well, for starters, a phone," he said. "I'll pick her up one of those cheap smart phones with a month-to-month plan. At least she'll have that. And she doesn't have decent fucking shampoo, for chrissake. I'm not saying let's take her to a spa, but we can afford to buy her some decent crap to make her a little more comfortable."

"Okay. Go ahead."

"Thanks." Kenny kissed him and started rooting through her clothes. Then he took out his phone.

"What are you doing?"

"Sizes," Kenny said. "I need to know what she wears."

"You said shampoo."

"I'll get her some PJs. Something loose. She barely has anything that doesn't look like she shouldn't be auditioning for a BSDM porn movie. That shit's not comfortable."

"Okay." They weren't rich, but they had disposable income. No, it wouldn't kill them to spend a little money on her.

"Besides," Kenny said, "I need to get some more stuff for dinner tonight. So I have to go out anyway."

In the living room, Nolan walked around to ask her if there was anything she needed, but she was already asleep.

Nolan sadly held the pillows. "I don't want to disturb her." He laid them on the coffee table where she could reach them if she woke up. He kissed Kenny. "Hurry back."

"I will." Kenny grabbed his keys and headed out to his car.

For chrissake, she didn't even have tampons or pads. There'd been exactly two of each in the bathroom at the apartment when they'd gone through it.

The rat bastard had even been rationing stuff like that.

He ended up at a Super Target he favored and grabbed a cart. Heading first to the clothing section, he found several cute and comfy pajama sets, some with pants and some with shorts, that would be loose and comfy on her. He added a couple of pairs of yoga pants in her size, hoping they'd be comfy for her. Some T-shirts with different funny retro logos and graphics on them, slightly oversized, a bathrobe, and two pairs of slippers.

He went through the health and beauty section and bought new everything he could think of, especially hair care. He didn't know if she'd even need it all, but he got styling gel, anti-frizz cream, three kinds of shampoo and conditioner for different hair types, razors, shaving gel, deodorant, tampons, pads—everything.

As a kid of a single mom, he'd long ago gotten over any squeamishness about what women bought for their personal needs. His mom had "the talk" with him when he was twelve and she caught him and a friend of his with his friend's dad's *Penthouse* magazine.

Yeah, he wasn't dumb. But he also silently thanked his mom for how she'd raised him.

He'd make sure he thanked her in person tonight.

And yes, he got food. But he also added some extras, like he found a cute Hello Kitty travel cup that had a straw. He didn't know if Betsy would even like Hello Kitty or not, but it made him smile, so maybe it'd make her smile, too. And yogurt, cottage cheese, some other soft foods he hoped she'd be able to eat all right until she healed up.

And chocolate.

Milk, and dark.

I need to find out if she has any allergies.

He'd almost reached the checkout line when he realized he hadn't picked up a phone. So back to electronics, where he grabbed one, having to pay for it there. He went for a slightly better phone. She could surf the Internet on it, tied into the Wi-Fi at their house for better speed.

It would be the first step of her reconnecting to others.

He was almost back to the checkout line when his cell phone rang.

Tilly wasted no time. "How is she?" she asked by way of greeting.

"I'm not home. Nolan's with her."

"Where are *you*?"

"Want me to start at the beginning?"

"Sure."

Kenny quickly detailed the morning for her.

"Wow, dude, I have a totally new level of respect for you. Buying tampons for a woman you barely know? Props."

"Gee, thanks."

"No, seriously. Good thinking. And if you want, we'll chip in for expenses."

"No, it's okay. We've got it."

"Leigh said they want to help her buy a car."

"Let's wait on that. She's overwhelmed right now. I don't know if she'll even accept it. Hey, come over and have dinner with us."

"Awesome, thanks. And we have your toybag. You want us to drop it off?"

"FYI, my mom's coming over for dinner tonight, too. Still want to join us?"

She snickered. "Of course I do. This should be interesting. You know I'm bringing Sir Fussypants and Cris, right? And can I bring anything?"

He heard Landry playfully protest the title in the background. "Yes, please," Kenny said. "Bring a side dish, if you'd like. We're eating at six, but get there a little after five, that would be even better."

"What gives? I know a set-up when I hear it."

He reminded her of his step-father.

"Ah. Oooh! So if he acts douchey, I can step in?"

"Be my guest." At this point, he'd love to see Tilly give Dennis a run for his homophobic money.

"You know what? I really like you. You do anything to fuck up my opinion of you, I'm liable to get upset."

"I promise, I'll do my best not to disappoint you."

"Cool. See you at five."

Kenny hung up and wheeled back around to return to the grocery section.

He'd need more food.

Chapter Six

In her dreams, Betsy was trapped in a nightmarish maze, the chain painfully banging on her right ankle as she ran through the labyrinth, always pulled up short just before what looked like a safe exit, forced to turn around and try another way.

Always with thunderous footsteps just behind her, Jack's harsh breathing, his threats of what he'd do to her.

She startled awake and let out a yelp of pain as she nearly rolled off the couch. Kenny, who'd apparently been sitting in an easy chair, dove to catch her, keeping her from hitting the floor.

Unable to help it, both from the pain and emotions, she burst into tears.

"I'm sorry," she said.

"Hey, why are you apologizing?" He helped her back into a more comfortable position, tucking pillows behind her head.

"This totally upends your lives."

"We're okay," he said. "We wouldn't have volunteered if we didn't want you here."

"And, honestly?" Nolan said from somewhere behind them. "You couldn't be by yourself right now. You couldn't get out of bed without help this morning. Don't be in a hurry to leave."

"What the hell happened to me?" she tearfully asked. "How did I let myself get into that situation?"

"We're all human," Kenny said as he sat on the coffee table. "We all make mistakes in the name of love."

"I thought I was so smart," she said. "I thought I knew what to watch out for. He had a job, he said all the right things, did all the right things."

"And that's what predators do," Kenny said. "They learn how to do those things. You were probably a challenge for him because you weren't some weak woman throwing yourself at him."

"I wasn't enough of a challenge, obviously," she darkly said. "I never should have played with him. I should have waited."

Nolan walked around the end of the couch to join Kenny. "Did he pressure you to play?"

"No, and that's exactly it! I asked him to play after we'd met a few times and talked. He didn't ask me. I knew that was a warning sign, if someone pressured you to play."

Nolan shrugged. "Predators improve their hunting skills, unfortunately."

"The sad thing is, I thought I sucked at vanilla relationships. I mean, they were nice guys, right? But it was…boring. Like there was always something missing. I just lost interest. When I discovered BDSM it all clicked home what I'd been needing. But even when I dated vanilla guys, I didn't hesitate to break up with a guy if he got too controlling or wanted too much, too fast. How ironic is *that*?"

"Again, predators are cunning," Kenny said. "It's their raison d'être. It's kind of what they get off on doing."

"Anything from Ed yet on bail?"

"He hasn't been arraigned yet," Nolan said. "In about an hour or so."

"So, here's another thing," Kenny said. "Tilly and her guys are coming over for dinner."

"Okay."

"And my mom."

"Oh." She let out a sigh. "I'll stay in my room then."

"No, that's not what I meant. We want you to eat with us. You're why Tilly and her guys are coming over. My mom's husband might be with her, but doubtful." Kenny and Nolan exchanged a glance. "We're going to tell my mom the full truth about us, and about who you are, tonight. We'd been talking about maybe getting married, and all this stuff made us realize how short life is and not to waste it."

"I'm happy for you," she said, feeling a little wistful. "That's great."

"Thanks," Nolan said. "We've already decided we're not going to tell anyone where you're staying, except the people who were there last night. If you decide later to tell anyone, that's up to you. For now, it's probably safer if we keep your location secret."

"Agreed." She winced as she tried to sit up by herself. These guys were so nice, so sweet.

So safe.

It would be tempting to let herself stay here too long, and she knew that.

Right now, she'd settle for being able to go to the bathroom by herself. "I hate to ask for help, but I need to get up."

The men rose as one. They were a lot alike despite their differences in appearance. Nolan, with his blond hair and blue eyes, a couple of inches taller than Kenny, who had short brown hair and brown eyes. Together, they got her on her feet and down the hall to the bathroom.

This time, at least, she was able to go by herself. And she avoided looking in the mirror when she washed her hands. When she turned, she spotted a bunch of new stuff on the shelf over the toilet, things that hadn't been there before.

Girlie stuff.

She turned to stare at them, where they stood in the doorway with guilty looks. "When did you go shopping?" she asked.

"After you zonked out," Kenny said. "If I didn't get the right stuff, let me know. I picked you up some pajamas and things, too."

Her one good eye watered. "It's perfect. Thanks. I appreciate it." She reached over, ripped open the box holding the deodorant, and reached under her shirt to apply some. "I had to use his. He wouldn't buy me any of my own." She replaced the cap and set it on the shelf. "I took stuff like this for granted before. I can't remember the last time I went shopping. I had to give him a list of stuff I needed, and he would buy it, *if* he felt like it. It was like I had to earn it."

When she turned, the dark expressions on the men's faces startled her. "What?"

"Sorry," Nolan quietly said. "Just that if we'd known he was being this shitty to you, we would have stepped in a lot sooner to try to help you out. A lot of us would have."

"It's my own fault for not saying anything and not leaving sooner. Well, it's my fault for letting him do this to me in the first place." She managed a glance in the mirror. "The worst part? I was raised not to tolerate this kind of abuse. I think that's why it took me so long to find BDSM and accept it. Then I threw myself into it wholeheartedly and got my heart ripped out in the process."

They got her situated back on the couch, this time sitting up. Nolan brought her more ibuprofen.

"When do I have to go back to get my stitches out?" she asked.

"You don't," Kenny said. "You were probably too out of it last night to understand all of that. They'd already given you a pain shot by then. They're dissolvable stitches. If you have swelling or infection, you have to go back. Otherwise, you're good. Well, other than the head injury."

At least the nausea had faded. Likely due to being able to eat. "I promise, when I'm feeling better, I'll start helping with chores."

"Stop," Nolan said. "Seriously, we mean it. We get it, you're not a mooch. Message received." He smiled. "Think of this as a very hard-earned vacation for a few days, okay?"

She nodded.

"Any ideas what to do about a job?" Kenny asked.

"No. I'll need to get a job so I can get a car. I doubt the place I worked will hire me back."

"Why's that?" Nolan asked.

"It was a real estate office. They've probably filled my position."

"Wouldn't hurt to ask."

"I will." Sadness settled over her. "I thought I'd met Dom Dashing. Instead, he was a Master Baiter."

Kenny snickered. "That's a good one. At least your sense of humor's still intact."

"About the only thing I have left that's still truly mine," she said. "And even then, he tried to beat that out of me, too."

* * * *

Ed called back a little later on Kenny's phone. "I have good news and bad news."

"Start with the bad," Kenny said as he walked into the living room and sat on the end of the couch.

"He's pleading not guilty, and the judge set his bail at one hundred thousand dollars."

"Dammit. What's the good news?"

"He didn't make bail. He doesn't have the money. And Tony got into that computer, which led us to doing a little looking around. We were able to access his online bank account. He's only got about a thousand dollars in his account. So he's going to be sitting right where he is for a while. He can't afford bail. And before you ask, no, we can't transfer the money out. She's not on the account. That would be fully illegal, and get her in trouble if we did it."

Kenny gave a very worried-looking Betsy a thumbs-up, triggering a sigh of relief from her. "That is good news, though," Kenny said.

Nolan appeared from the kitchen. "What?"

"Didn't make bail," Kenny said.

Nolan pumped his fist and sat in one of the easy chairs to listen in.

"I'm going to file for the restraining order to be made permanent tomorrow," Ed said. "Is there anything else we need to get for her out of the apartment?"

"Let me ask." He turned to her. "Did we get everything you need last night?"

"Well, everything that's technically mine. If he can't get out of jail, I wouldn't mind going in and getting stuff I'll have to replace that he made me get rid of, like dishes and stuff."

Kenny spoke to Ed. "What's the legalities of clearing out the rest of the apartment?"

"She was a resident there. Her driver's license lists that address. Legally, she can do what she wants with the contents. The police have released the scene. And I have a list of volunteers ready to go get everything else."

"Do it, please."

"Kel's got an empty unit over at the complex. We'll move it there for now. The Collins brothers said it'll take less than an hour to do."

"Do we need to bring her over?" Kenny asked.

"Not unless she wants to come. We'll leave any men's clothing behind. I'm sure the landlord will appreciate not having to empty the place."

"Thanks. Keep us posted." She motioned for the phone. "Hold on." Kenny passed it to her.

"Ed?"

"Yeah, honey?"

"Please tell everyone how much I appreciate all of this. I'll find a way to pay them back somehow."

"You pay them back by healing your body and making a full recovery with your life."

* * * *

Tilly and her men arrived at a quarter till five. Nolan no sooner had the door open than she swooped in past him with a peck on the cheek, aiming straight for Betsy on the couch.

Landry smiled. "Long time, no see." He carried Kenny and Nolan's bag and set it just inside the door.

"Yeah, tell me about it." He reached for the covered casserole dish Cris was carrying. "Ed said they've emptied the apartment except for Jack's clothes."

"Good," Landry said with a satisfied nod. "That'll be a nice surprise for him to return to, if he ever makes bail."

As Nolan carried the dish into the kitchen, he spotted Tilly sitting on the couch next to Betsy, her arm around Betsy's shoulders.

He suspected Tilly would practically glue herself to Betsy whenever possible. Her and Eliza both. Tilly would soon be starting work as Leigh's assistant out in LA at their production company, and Eliza would have to stand in for their group's de facto momma bear.

"So what's the plan, man?" Tilly asked Kenny as he joined them in the living room.

Nolan returned from the kitchen. "I think that depends in part on whether or not Dennis comes with Mom for dinner."

Tilly shrugged. "We going for full honesty, here? Or just 'common friends,' or what?"

Nolan looked to Kenny. This was his mom. He knew he had his own revelations he'd have to go through with his family, but he wouldn't make this decision for his partner.

"Full honesty," Kenny said. "At first I wasn't going to talk about the BDSM stuff, but you know what? If I'm going to get it all out on the table, I'm going to feel a lot better."

"Cool," Tilly said. She glared at Landry, who looked like he was about to speak. "And yes, I will behave myself, Sir. Fussypants."

Cris snickered. "One of these days, you're going to say that to him and he's going to haul off and spank you in the bad way."

She stuck her tongue out at Cris. "No, he won't. Because he lurrrrves me." She blew Landry a kiss.

Nolan was relieved to see Betsy attempt a smile. "I hope my appearance doesn't scare the crap out of your mom," she said. "I look horrible."

"This might sound wrong," Kenny said, "but I'm going to put it out there anyway. I'm honestly hoping she feels so badly for you that she sort of glosses over the whole BDSM revelation. That, and that we're sometimes poly with a woman."

Tilly gasped. "You two sometimes partner up with women?" she said, sounding totally surprised. "I had *no* idea."

Now Betsy laughed. She patted Tilly on the leg. "Tilly, please. Lying doesn't suit you. I swear that I will not get involved in any other relationship unless you and-or Eliza have signed off on it first. But it's way too soon for you to try matchmaking, okay? I don't even have a damn car. I just want my life back first."

"Well, can't blame a Domme for trying, can you?"

"No, and I love you for it."

"Oh, she has a phone," Kenny said, getting up to retrieve it from where he'd left it charging in their bedroom.

"She does?" Tilly whipped hers out. "Cool, what's the number?"

"I do?" Betsy asked.

"I bought you one," Kenny called over his shoulder.

"What?"

Nolan caught the hint of fear in her voice and called him back. "Kenny, wait." Nolan arched an eyebrow at her. "It's not an expensive phone or an expensive plan. But we're doing this for you for two reasons. One, you need a phone of your own. Consider the phone and the first two months a gift. Hopefully by that point you'll be able to afford to pay for it yourself. If not, we'll give you two more months as an early Christmas gift."

Her left eye closed, a tear squeezing out from under the lid as she nodded.

Tilly's voice dropped, her tone tender. "Betsy, you're not the first woman to end up in this situation. The difference here is you have people who love you and want to help you. Let us help you. Please?"

Betsy nodded again. "Thank you."

Nolan nodded for Kenny to get the phone. He brought it back, showing her how to use it. Tilly immediately set to work programming a bunch of numbers into it for her, including hers and her men's numbers, Eliza, Tony, Shayla, Ross and Loren, Ed—everyone. Kenny had already programmed his and Nolan's cell and work numbers into it for her to have.

After Tilly returned it to her, Betsy stared at it for a long moment, then handed it to Tilly. "Take a picture of me," she quietly said.

Tilly's brow furrowed. "Uh, why?"

"Because I never want to forget this. I want a picture of how I look right now, so if I ever start to do something stupid again, even after I've forgotten how badly this hurts, even after I've moved on and have my life and independence back, I want to be able to look at my face and remember why I can't fuck up this badly ever again."

Chapter Seven

Kenny wasn't the least bit surprised when he heard a car door shut two minutes before six and glanced out the front window to see his mom walking up their driveway.

Alone.

He already had the front door open when she stepped onto the porch. "Hi, Mom."

"Hi, sweetie. Extra guests for dinner?"

He took the red velvet cake she'd made from her. "Yeah, that's…complicated."

"Compli—" Her jaw snapped shut when she spotted Betsy sitting on the couch.

"Mom, it's a long story, and I promise you, you'll get all of it." He made a quick round of introductions while Nolan came and took the cake from him.

His mom walked around the coffee table to sit on the other end of the couch next to Betsy. "I hope the son of a bitch who did this to you is in jail!"

"He is, Mom," Kenny assured her.

He started with the quick version, that Betsy called Tilly for help, and a bunch of them rushed in to provide said help.

When he finished that part, his mom glanced at Tilly, her men, then back to him. "Okay. So what aren't you telling me?"

Nolan had joined them out in the living room. "You know how that one night after dinner we had the TV on, and one of those commercials for the *Fifty Shades* movie played?" Kenny asked her.

"Yeah?"

"We all live it in real life."

The room went tomb-silent.

Kenny watched his mom as her gaze swiveled from him, to Betsy, to Nolan, then to Tilly and her guys. "So you three," she said, using a finger to indicate Tilly, Landry, and Cris, "are a…group?"

"Triad," Landry offered. "We're a poly triad. Tilly is my wife, and Cris is my slave, and we're all partners."

"And it's really complicated if we explain more than that," Tilly added, this time without any of her characteristic snark added for conversational flavor.

His mom nodded, then looked back at Kenny. "So, some of those women you and Nolan brought around before?"

He nodded. "They were women we were dating or playing with," he admitted.

"And her?" She pointed at Betsy. "No offense to any of you, but she looks like she should be in the hospital."

"I checked myself out of the ER last night," Betsy said. "Don't worry, right now, all I'm planning to do is survive long enough to look human again and get my life back."

"So the guy who beat you up…"

"I was a dummy who fell for a guy who suckered me in. Most guys are nice guys. Like Kenny and Nolan. Or Landry and Cris. They don't do this." She pointed at her own face. "This is abuse, and believe me, I know it."

"Okay." She seemed to be digesting that. Then, she looked at Kenny and shook a finger at him. "I ever hear of *you* doing something like *this* to anyone? You'll be dealing with me, young man."

Tilly snorted. "Don't worry. There wouldn't be enough left of him for you to deal with."

* * * *

Betsy didn't know if Kenny's mom was just that cool, or if Michelle was trying to act cool because Betsy knew she looked like complete and utter hell, but she didn't care. The woman was sweet and ordered Betsy and the others to call her "Mom."

She wouldn't dare argue.

"Well, I'm glad Dennis didn't come with me tonight," she said as they sat down to eat. "That would have made things even more interesting."

"So how is he?" Kenny asked.

Michelle shrugged. "Still sulking. I think he's upset that I didn't beg him to come with me tonight. I told him he could either act like an adult or get the hell out. I raised my child. I'm not raising another one. Especially when he's supposed to be a damned adult."

"I'm sorry, Mom," Kenny said. "We didn't realize he'd come home, or we would have been more careful."

She waved him off. "It's okay. It had to come out sooner or later. So, when do I get to plan you and Nolan's wedding?"

Betsy couldn't help but laugh as Kenny choked on the swallow of iced tea he'd been taking. "Mom!"

"Well? The secret's out now, right? Get married before the boneheads in Tallahassee figure out a way to stop it again."

"We still have to tell my parents," Nolan said. "I'm not sure how that will go."

Michelle nodded. "At least you boys have a supportive group of friends, if these three here—and Betsy—are any indication."

Betsy thought she might be able to sit there and avoid talking, but Michelle, who'd sat right next to her, pulled her into the conversation. "So, what are your next plans? What did you do for a living? Any job prospects?"

"I don't know yet. I'm going to work on my resume and talk to the real estate office where I worked before Jack made me quit. See if they're hiring or know of anyone who might be. From there..." She shrugged. "I'm not sure."

"No degree?"

"Just a two-year from community college for business. Bookkeeping, accounting, basic stuff. I couldn't afford a four-year school and didn't have the grades for a scholarship."

Michelle nodded. "Well, keep me posted. If you're familiar with real estate, have you done any property management?"

"Not really. Our office handled residential sales. Why?"

"One of the women in our office is moving in a few weeks. We're going to post the position sometime this week. We handle commercial and retail property management. Several business plazas, a mall, things like that. It's an administrative position. Starts at forty thousand a year, but you'll have to apply for it. I can't just give you the job because you're my son's friend."

Hope started to catch fire inside her. "Thank you! Yes, I'd love the chance to apply." It was a little more than she'd made at her last job, and she'd been living okay with that salary. Not high off the hog, but she'd had a tidy little apartment and a car that ran well and was paid off, with a few extra dollars to go to Venture or a movie every weekend, or to buy herself a nice dinner, if she wanted to.

"Okay. Then get me your resume as soon as you can. The sooner you can apply, the sooner we can get you in to interview. It'll be about two weeks or so before we start interviews."

"Thank you. I appreciate it." That would give her time to heal up reasonably well.

"I'll help you with your resume tomorrow," Tilly said. "I'll be over here before the guys leave for work and we'll do that."

"Thanks." She stared down at her plate while fighting the urge to cry. The kindness everyone had shown her...It was the polar opposite of the hell she'd just escaped from not even twenty-four hours ago.

This time yesterday, she'd been beaten and bloody and curled up on the couch, nearly unconscious, after a day of struggling to get the chain off her foot.

Michelle reached over and touched her shoulder. "Are you all right?"

"No, but I'm finally thinking maybe I'll reach that point sooner than I thought I would."

* * * *

Betsy said good-night to everyone and headed to bed right after dessert was served and Tilly had quickly examined her to make sure she was okay. She'd taken a couple of ibuprofen and needed to lie down. Her headache was back, along with all the other aches and pains, and she didn't want to admit to anyone how bad she was feeling.

With Michelle and Tilly there, she might just end up back in the hospital with no say in the matter. *Especially* if Tilly the nurse thought she wasn't doing well.

Then Betsy spotted the plastic shopping bags from the store on her bed. When she opened them, she stifled a sob.

Dammit, would she ever get control of her emotions again?

Yes, she remembered Kenny saying something about pajamas. And yes, they were in her sizes.

And they were adorable. One of them was covered with Hello Kitty, something she'd loved.

Jack never would have bought her anything he didn't see a real use for. Why'd she need PJs when she should sleep naked for him, anyway?

She was lucky he'd had a vasectomy years ago, but then a nagging thought struck her.

Maybe I need to get myself tested.

She didn't think he was cheating on her. He was usually far too strict about his time and hers to have any that wasn't really accounted for.

Well, except for his afternoons and nights as a bouncer at the bar.

But, add to the fact that he'd had a difficult time getting it up a lot of the time. So…probably not.

Just in case…

She added a trip to the county health department to her list of things to do at some point. She'd need a full STD/HIV panel done. And then again in six months.

Dammit.

She pulled the tags off the Hello Kitty PJs and carefully undressed, then pulled the PJs on.

Yes, perfect fit. Loose enough to be comfy.

Wincing, she slowly got into bed and pulled the sheet over herself, leaving the bedside lamp on again. But the PJs…

It was like falling asleep cloaked in kindness.

* * * *

Once Betsy's bedroom door softly closed behind her, Kenny watched as his mom's expression turned dark.

"I hope that guy gets serious jail time," she said.

"I hope he ends up cellmates with a three-hundred-pound nymphomaniac bodybuilder hung like an elephant," Tilly snarked.

"I used to have a friend, years ago," Michelle started, "who once confided she liked it when her husband spanked her. I understand that, I guess. But how does someone go from harmless play to *that*?" She pointed down the hallway, where Betsy had gone.

"They usually don't," Landry assured her. "He is an exception, fortunately."

"Well, like I told her, I can't promise her a job. But she can apply."

"I appreciate that, Mom."

"I'm sure when you left my house yesterday morning, you were worried about something like that happening to me, hmm?"

"Honestly? Yeah. We were."

She smiled. "Dennis might hold radically different political views than I do, but believe me, he would never lay a finger on me." Her smile faded. "When we were dating, we were once talking and joking around somehow, and I smiled and told him if any man ever hit me, he'd better never go to sleep around me. *Ever*. Because he would regret it."

Kenny sat up. He couldn't believe his mom saying something like that. "What'd he say?"

"He laughed, then realized I wasn't kidding." She took a sip of iced tea. "I dated a few jerks when you were younger. None I brought home, fortunately. One of them was a man who tried to intimidate me with force. He didn't actually hit me, but I'm sure had I not put a stop to things when I did that he probably would have."

"What happened?"

"Oh, he got a little rough with me when he tried to get me to have sex with him. I got loud in return. Then he claimed he was just kidding around. So before I left, I went to use the bathroom. I'd swiped a bottle of Super Glue I spotted in his kitchen. I filled the bathroom door lock with it before going back into the living room, and left the bathroom door closed, and locked."

Kenny's eyes widened as Tilly cackled with glee and gave her a high-five.

"What the hell?" Kenny said. "You never told me that!"

"Of course not. You were nine or ten when it happened. Really young."

"What happened later when he figured it out?" Tilly asked.

She shrugged. "I don't know. But I'm sure when he left to go to work the next morning he probably wasn't very happy, either."

"Why?" Kenny asked.

She took another sip of her tea. "Because I also filled the locks on his car doors and trunk with glue when I left. I had a rule to always drive myself. I had you to think about, to make sure I came home safely. So I waited until I knew he wasn't watching and did it."

“Did he accuse you of it?”

“He never called me again. Which was fine by me.”

“I’ve gotta say,” Tilly told Kenny, “I am *totally* fangirling your mom right now. Can I be your adopted sister?”

Chapter Eight

After all the dishes were done and everyone had left for the evening, Kenny and Nolan headed to their bedroom. With the door securely closed behind them, Kenny pulled Nolan into his arms for a long, scorching kiss. Nolan was only two inches taller than his own six one, and their bodies seemed built to fit together perfectly.

"Can I redeem the rain check on the fucking part of last night's activities?" Kenny asked when he lifted his lips from Nolan's.

Nolan smiled down at him, his blue eyes looking like a dark ocean's depths in this light. "I think that could be arranged."

"Good." Kenny started backing him toward their bed. "Because I'm in a serious need of a good, hard fucking from you."

Nolan grabbed him, spun around, and shoved Kenny back, hard, onto the bed, pouncing on top of him. "Like this?"

"That's a good start."

Nolan grabbed his lover's hands, lacing fingers with him, and pinned Kenny's hands over his head against the mattress. He leaned in close, body stretched over Kenny's, lips inches above his.

"Then prepare to be well and truly fucked tonight, buddy."

Kenny squeezed his hands and the look of vulnerability that swept through his lover's brown gaze took Nolan's breath away. They were pretty much equals. Yes, they took turns bottoming in bed, and sometimes for play, but they were both definitely Dominant men.

He suspected the revelations Kenny's mom had made at dinner had started Kenny's brain whirring again, worrying about her when compared to Betsy's situation.

Slanting his mouth over Kenny's, Nolan crushed his lover's lips under his, fucking Kenny's mouth with his tongue and drawing a soft moan from Kenny.

Under him, he felt Kenny's cock harden against him in response to his own erection. He sat up, still pinning Kenny's hands over his head.

"Don't move," he ordered. Then he sat back, Kenny's hands remaining where he'd left them.

He swung off Kenny and left the bed, quickly stripping before grabbing a towel, lube, and a condom. He returned to the bed and dropped the items onto the mattress before he reached in and started unfastening Kenny's shorts.

Kenny remained where Nolan had left him, staring up at him, waiting.

Getting Kenny's shorts and briefs down and off him, Nolan shoved the man's shirt up over his nipples. Sliding his hands up the man's smooth abs, he leaned in and licked a trail from navel to nipples, back and forth, nipping at them, deliberately positioning his body between Kenny's legs and forcing them wider apart so his lover's cock rubbed against his bare flesh.

This would be a hard and fast fuck, for sure, so he wanted to drag the foreplay out a little. They enjoyed cuddling, no doubt, but sometimes they wanted—needed—raw, animalistic rutting that could sate the sadistic needs both men suppressed when there wasn't another ready outlet.

And right now, both of them wanted to beat the shit out of Jack Bourke, something that wouldn't happen.

So they'd fuck the hell out of each other instead and enjoy it just the same.

It was always fun when they had a woman between them as a third. Especially if she was a masochist. Then they could unleash primal play that would always leave her satisfied and smiling, and leave the men's darker urges happily sated.

Neither had an interest in forcing someone to comply or submit. The person had to want it. Which was why neither man minded play with the other. They understood the need, knew how to appease it.

Enjoyed the reciprocity.

And hell, they could really fight against the other one if they wanted, without worrying about someone getting hurt. It was fun, it was furious, and it was fucking amazing once they wore themselves out and collapsed on the other end of the play.

Nolan slid down Kenny's body, grabbing his cock and wrapping his lips around it, flicking at the slit with his tongue while Kenny lifted his head and watched.

Down Kenny's shaft, Nolan laved his tongue over Kenny's cock, his balls, sucking first one and then the other into his mouth while Kenny's hips started rocking, trying to gain traction against Nolan's grip around his cock.

Pre-cum oozed from the tip of Kenny's cock, sweetly salty, rolling down Nolan's tongue as he sucked on it and swirled his tongue around the head.

He continued the torture, his own cock throbbing and leaking, his balls aching for release, knowing he wanted to work Kenny almost to the brink of explosion when Nolan finally shoved his cock up him. Because he knew he wouldn't, couldn't last long inside the man as horny as he now felt, too.

Cupping Kenny's sac in his other palm, Nolan slowly stroked his lover's shaft, enjoying the way Kenny's cock grew even harder under his fingers. Delicious desperation filled Kenny's eyes as he stared down his body at Nolan.

Yes, *this*. This is what Nolan loved, having that willingly given control, the trust.

For a split second, Nolan imagined what Betsy might look like wearing a similar desperately helpless expression before he shoved it out of his mind. Totally inappropriate right now, not to mention he didn't want them landing in the middle of a messy emotional situation. Helping her by letting her live with them was one thing.

Fantasizing about her when she was asleep in the other room and still looking like a human punching bag?

Doooucheeey.

He sat up and lifted Kenny's knees, shoving them up and back against the other man's chest. "Hold them."

Kenny finally moved his hands, hooking them behind his knees to keep himself in position.

The Nolan grabbed the towel and slid it under him before reaching for the lube. He made sure to lock gazes with Kenny as he squirted some of the cool gel onto his fingers and started working it into the man's rim.

Kenny's cock twitched as a soft moan escaped him.

"Yeah, that's it. Make a little noise for me, baby. Gonna get you ready and then fuck what's mine."

That only made Kenny's cock twitch and throb more, another drop of pre-cum oozing from the slit and sliding down onto Kenny's abs.

Long ago, they'd learned anything goes with role-play in bed. Tomorrow, it might be Kenny fucking Nolan and making him beg for it while telling Kenny he was his willing bitch. It was fun, a fluid power exchange they didn't exactly consider switchy like Abbey and Gilo, or even Tilly and her guys. Similar, but different. Theirs was more role-play, with them both remaining dominant.

Once he had three fingers easily sliding into Kenny's channel, he wiped his hand and rolled on the condom. After slathering his shaft with lube, he pressed the head of his cock against Kenny's rim.

"Beg me."

"Please, fuck me," Kenny gasped. "Please pound that cock inside me."

He grabbed Kenny's ankles and slung them over his shoulders, leaning in but still not breaching his ass. "Harder."

"Please," Kenny said. "I need your cock."

"Still not feeling it."

"Goddammit, please fuck my—"

With one hard, deep thrust, Nolan slammed his cock all the way inside his lover, enjoying the sound of Kenny's moaning gasp of pleasure. "Hands over your head," Nolan ordered.

Kenny immediately complied.

He reached between Kenny's legs and wrapped his fingers around the man's cock. A steady stream of pre-cum now flowed from the slit, and he slicked the juices up and down Kenny's cock, slowly pumping with his hand.

"Should I get you off? Or should I fuck you and leave you hard and horny all night, hmm?" Nolan teased.

"Please get me off!"

"Maybe I should fuck you, then get a butt plug and shove it inside you and make you blow me in the morning before I let you come."

"No, please make me come!"

In their years together, they'd each learned the other's quirks, weak points, and triggers, good and bad.

Like this, alone together, when he was in the mood to be, Kenny liked it when Nolan pushed him, hard and deep, down into a bottomy headspace. Never truly submissive, but it always made Kenny come harder when he wanted it like this.

And he could tell Kenny *really* wanted it like this.

Nolan slowly withdrew his cock until just the head still remained inside Kenny's ass before taking another hard, pounding thrust into him.

In his hand, Kenny's cock throbbed, close to exploding.

"Maybe I should just make you my little bitch for the week," Nolan growled. "Keep you edging all week. Make you play with yourself at lunch but not come. Make you blow me every morning and every night."

Another thrust, and he closed his fingers even more firmly around Kenny's cock. "Make you present your ass to me for fucking, hands and knees and lubed, ready from having a butt plug in all day."

"No, please let me come!"

Nolan started fucking him slowly, stroking Kenny's cock in time with his thrusts. He wanted to time it just right, so he could feel Kenny coming, feel the way his ass fisted his cock just before he blew his own load.

"You come all over my hand, you're going to have to lick it up. You know that, right?"

"Anything!"

He started stroking Kenny's cock faster, a little twist around the head at the top of each stroke, gathering more of his juices with every swipe. He knew Kenny was close to exploding. He picked up the pace of his own fucking, now short, deep thrusts, hitting Kenny right in the sweet spot with each jab, driving him harder and closer to release.

"Then I guess you'd better come before I do if you don't want to spend a week being tortured."

He felt Kenny trying to rock his hips, but the way Nolan had him pinned, all he could do was lay there and look helpless and horny, out of his mind with need and desire.

When Nolan felt the first spurts of cum from Kenny's cock, he picked up the pace of his strokes with his hand, struggling to hold back as Kenny's ass started squeezing his cock. And then Kenny threw his head back, eyes closed, a long, satisfied moan escaping him and nearly triggering Nolan's release as Kenny's hot juices covered his hand.

As he started fucking him harder, faster now, long, pounding strokes, Kenny grabbed Nolan's hand from his cock and started sucking on it, licking it, looking up into his eyes and that was when Nolan finally let loose. His balls throbbed, pumping, filling the condom even as Kenny stared up at him and licked his own juices from Nolan's fingers.

Breathing heavy, Nolan fell still, curling his fingers around Kenny's as he started laughing. "Damn, I needed that."

Kenny grinned, even as he still had one of Nolan's fingers between his lips. "Me, too," he mumbled.

He finally managed to get Kenny to release his hand. After lowering the man's legs, he leaned in and kissed him. "Shower?"

"Yeah."

A minute later, they were holding each other under the warm spray, kissing, relaxing, coming down from their respective head spaces.

"Love you, man," Kenny said. "And even if you never want to tell your parents—"

Nolan silenced him with a gentle finger pressed against his lips. "Love you, too." He sighed. "And yeah, I am going to tell my parents. I have to. Because I'm not going to hold off marrying the guy I love just because I'm afraid of what they're going to say. Life's too damn short."

Kenny slid his hand behind Nolan's neck, cupping it, holding him in place for another long, tender kiss. Pressing his forehead to Nolan's, he whispered, "Marry me."

"Yes," Nolan whispered back. "Marry *me*."

Kenny kissed him. "Yes."

Chapter Nine

Monday morning, Betsy laid in bed, her left eye open, her right eye barely able to squint just a little.

She'd take the win.

It was nearly seven in the morning, and she couldn't believe she'd slept so late. Jack had to be up at 6:15 every morning to get ready for work, meaning she had to be up, too, fixing his lunch, cooking his breakfast.

Everything.

Failure to get up on time meant one cane stroke for every minute. The only time she was allowed to sleep in was on Saturdays and Sundays when he did.

Freedom.

And more than a little self-loathing settled within her as she stared at the strange furnishings belonging to the men, furnishings that she knew would quickly grow familiar.

No, she hadn't been living a ritzy lifestyle before Jack. But she'd let Jack order her into getting rid of most of her belongings when she moved in with him.

Or he'd basically confiscated them, like her computer, and declared them his.

Once she moved into her own place, she would eventually start replacing the things she'd given up. And the things of Jack's that the men had retrieved for her, like dishes, and pots and pans, that were Jack's. Oh, she'd use them, all right, for now.

But eventually, everything she owned would be hers and hers alone. She'd be damned if she'd ever let another man do this to her.

What the hell *was wrong with me? How did I get here?*

It was something she'd asked herself a lot lately.

Especially over the past couple of weeks.

Usually as she'd sit there and stare at the damn chain on her ankle and try to figure out how the hell to get it off.

In the beginning, Jack had seemed like a nice guy. Said the right things. She'd trusted him, allowed a little more trust. She didn't play with him alone. She met him in public. He never pressured her to play alone, encouraged her to talk to others. But since he was new to the area, and said he wasn't really active in local groups up north, there hadn't been much to ask about.

No one had anything bad to say about him down here, that she'd heard. It seemed like Tilly wasn't fond of him, but to be honest, there were a few people who didn't like Tilly. To her friends, she was fiercely loyal and protective, and that sometimes got lost in translation when dealing with someone like Jack. Someone who didn't know her or her history.

That Tilly wasn't fond of him should have been enough for Betsy. But he'd charmed several others, played with a few at the club, and no one seemed to have anything bad to say about him locally.

Tilly's grumbles mostly quieted as he didn't actually do anything that raised red flags.

So Betsy had allowed him into her life a little. First, just for play. At the club. Then orgasm play. Then they talked about maybe a training collar.

And then…

Then one day she found herself staring at a damn chain locked around her right ankle and trying to figure out how the hell she'd let *that* happen.

It was like a vicious carousel she'd managed to get on, but before she could get off, before she'd realized that it wasn't populated by beautiful ponies and lions, and instead held horrific monsters, it was spinning too fast for her to jump off without risking her very life. At that point, she'd held on as best she could and prayed for a chance to get off the ride.

She'd had no doubts that if Jack had realized she'd gotten the chain off that afternoon, after beating her, the next step would have been him chaining it around her neck. He'd once "joked" about doing that.

Maybe that had been his plan all along, to see how she'd tolerate the thing at first and work his way up to that.

Why the hell *did I tolerate it?*

There were plenty of times she could have waited for him to go to work and then screamed for help until someone called 911 to report it.

But he'd said he had spies.

And she'd believed him. He was crazy enough.

And if one of them had called *him* instead of the cops…

Yes, fear. Flat-out fear.

And stupidity, but that had kicked in after the fact, once she knew she was finally safe.

I have to get up.

The rest of her life lay ahead of her. She was only thirty-two and had a lot of good years. Yes, she had some rebuilding to do, but she would do it.

To do it meant she needed to start now, be independent.

Including getting out of damn bed by herself.

At least her headache felt like maybe it had finally abated. And she didn't feel dizzy.

She just…hurt like fucking hell.

Slowly, she log-rolled onto her right side, pausing to breathe through the pain. It wouldn't get any worse from this point out, only better. He would never beat her again. If she could take it now, it would get easier to take, day by day, until her injuries fully healed.

Working carefully, she pushed herself up into a sitting position with her legs hanging over the edge of the bed.

Hey, look at that!

It was a small accomplishment, but to her she might as well have finished a marathon.

Leaning carefully, she stretched and reached for one of the shopping bags still setting on the end of the bed, where she'd seen a bathrobe last night. Fishing it out, she yanked the tag off and pulled it on before forcing herself into a standing position. Yes, trying to brush her hair would suck. That was something she still wasn't sure she could do by herself today.

Maybe Tilly can help me shave my legs.

Turning, she dug one of the two pairs of slippers out of the bag and dropped them onto the floor, then slid her feet into them.

Clothes. It felt good to have *comfy* clothes.

Fuck, it felt good to have *clothes*, period, to freely *choose* to wear them.

Jack had required her to be naked most of the time.

She'd forgotten the luxury of having comfy, cute clothes to wear. Nothing fancy, but PJs that made her feel good. Her new phone lay on the dresser, plugged in and charging. She slipped it into the pocket of her robe.

Just that simple act felt good. Freeing.

Shuffling, she made it to the bedroom door and got it opened. As if equipped with radar, Nolan and Kenny rushed down the hall from the kitchen.

"Are you okay?" Nolan asked.

"You didn't call for us," Kenny said.

They both wore shorts, no shirts, and looked adorable.

She managed a smile. "Thanks, guys. I've got to do this by myself eventually."

"But are you okay?" Nolan asked.

"I'm vertical. Does that count?"

They moved aside for her as she started what felt like a forever journey across the hall toward the bathroom. "Oh, guys?"

"Yeah?" they said.

She made a half-turn so she could look at them. "Thank you for the PJs and stuff. They're really cute. I love Hello Kitty."

The broad, beaming smile that lit Kenny's face sent off warning bells inside her. Not because of him, but because she knew it'd be too damn easy to fall into the trap of wanting to keep making him smile like that.

Sort of the way Jack had trapped her.

She wasn't so stupid that she was going to lock the bathroom door. Just in case she had pushed herself too far, too fast, and got in trouble and couldn't get back up again. Fortunately, she managed to use the bathroom by herself this time. The men were waiting for her outside when she emerged.

"Coffee's ready," Nolan said.

She smiled. "Can I have it in my Hello Kitty cup, please?"

"Absolutely. Ice?"

"Yes, please."

"I was hoping you'd like that cup," Kenny said. "I thought it was cute and fun."

"Believe me, I need all the cute and fun I can get."

"Are you okay to walk?" Kenny asked.

She took stock of her injuries. She still hurt. A lot. Including her right ankle. "I wouldn't refuse holding onto your arm."

He held it out for her, and it was nice to have the choice of whether to take it or not.

Well, not really a choice, because as she moved more, her pain was growing, and she knew it would only be a matter of time before she quickly hit her wall in terms of what she could do that day.

Kenny got her seated on the sofa and Nolan brought her water, ibuprofen, and then went back for her coffee.

"Can we make you breakfast?" Kenny said.

"When is Tilly getting here?"

"Any minute."

"I don't want to make you guys late for work."

"It's all right. We don't mind."

"How about some instant oatmeal?" Nolan called from the kitchen.

"All right. Thank you."

"Your right eye looks a little less swollen today," Kenny said.

She had avoided looking in the mirror again while in the bathroom. "I think it is. I can squint out of it a little bit."

Outside, she heard a car drive up.

"And there's Tilly," Kenny said. He went to the front door and had it open by the time she swept up the walk and through the door, not even breaking stride to speak to Kenny.

"Good, you're up. We have a lot to do today." She had a computer case and a small tote bag slung over her shoulder.

"You look prepared for battle," Betsy said.

"You have a shower yet?"

"No."

Nolan brought Betsy a bowl of oatmeal. "Here you go. Let her eat first, Tilly."

"Sorry. Eat first. Shower. Then we're going to do some stuff and work on your resume."

Kenny walked over. "The printer is on the desk in the office. We'll turn it on and leave you the Wi-Fi password. It should show up as a networked printer.

"Excellent. Oh, and hi, Kenny. Hi, Nolan. Pardon my lack of manners, but I'm on a mission."

Kenny smiled. "No problem. I could sort of tell."

"And you two don't worry. I'll be here until you guys get home, at least."

That meant one more person whose life she was interrupting.

*Dis*rupting. "I'm sorry," Betsy softly said.

Tilly frowned. "For what?"

"For getting myself into this mess in the first place."

"Yeah, well, listen. We all do stupid shit from time to time. We're human. Learning from it and not repeating it is the key there. Sometimes, we have to touch the stove."

"I feel like I shoved my whole face against it," she admitted.

Tilly put down her stuff and sat next to her on the couch, her tone now totally lacking snark.

"What we do," she said, "isn't exactly in the realm of the norm. We take risks. Sometimes, really big risks. The vanilla population doesn't always take those same risks. Sometimes, they do. Sometimes there are vanilla guys who beat the crap out of—and even kill—their partners. This isn't solely a kinky-person problem.

"But I want you to promise me that you won't let this experience turn you hard and cold, either. To take away your ability to eventually trust again. I've been there, done that, and honey? Let me tell you something. That's a cold, dark, lonely fucking place I wouldn't wish my worst enemy into. Having come out on the other side of it, I can tell you, it was absolutely no fun. Unfortunately, at the time, it was the easier choice to make. So please, don't make that easy choice to lock yourself away out of fear and regret and mistrust. Deal?"

Betsy had listened to all of this as her left eye stared down into her bowl of oatmeal. "I'll try," she whispered, "but I can't promise."

Right now, she felt torn between wanting to burn down the world and bury herself in a hole. She understood, logically, that those feelings, too, would pass. But for now, her emotions were freely pinballing around inside her, no longer restrained.

"All I'm asking is that you try," Tilly said.

Betsy nodded.

Tilly left her alone for a few minutes to go talk to the men in the kitchen. Betsy didn't turn when she heard them walk down the hall, followed by the sound of a bedroom door opening. The office, if she had to guess. She really hadn't had a tour of their house.

Not that she'd been in much of a mental or physical condition to get one.

Tilly's words still rang through her mind. When she thought back to her previous relationships, she'd guarded herself. Smartly, yes, in retrospect. Still, back then, she'd willingly stepped onto and off of a very slow-moving carousel filled with all the sweet and pretty—and safe, and *boring*—characters one would expect of such a ride.

Nothing with teeth that could bite, or claws that could rend.

Nothing like the monster she'd escaped from.

A kind of functional numbness had set in since she'd limped out the door of that apartment Saturday night. Instinctively, she wanted to cry, to scream, to rage, and yet she stared down at those emotions from some higher vantage point, as if looking at a different person.

She was a different person.

Damn sure wasn't who she thought she was.

The others returned a few minutes later. "Well, I think I can work that thing," Tilly joked as she reached for her computer bag and pulled her laptop out. "I'll make sure I can access the Internet and printer while they're still here, though."

"Do you need anything else before we get our showers?" Kenny asked Betsy.

"I'm good. Thanks."

Tilly had her laptop open and booting up. "They're good men," Tilly said, still in that non-snarky tone Betsy knew she'd need to get used to.

She suspected this was the real Tilly, the one Landry and Cris got to see, or some of her closest friends, but a side of her that Betsy had never experienced before this.

The Tilly she knew could be prickly, frank, snarky, and while never deliberately mean and on the offensive without damn good provocation, was someone who never hesitated to throw herself to the frontlines of the battle in defense of the people and friends she considered her responsibility.

"Yeah," Betsy said. "I feel badly I'm putting them out."

Tilly looked at her. "Stop. Now. We get it. I'm not trying to be a bitch, but we understand you feel badly about this. The next step is you need to move forward and not wallow. Show them your gratitude by kicking ass and taking names."

"Is that your motivational speech?"

"Yeah, and I think it still needs some work." She smiled. "Look, I'm not saying this is going to be easy. At all. I feel more than a little guilty that I didn't push you harder to wait to get involved with that guy. I feel badly that I didn't personally start looking into him sooner the way Tony did later on. I feel badly that I didn't try to reach out to you more often after you ended up with the guy. I feel damned guilty that I could see the signs of abuse there and I didn't step in a lot sooner and say whoa, what the fuck."

Tilly tapped on her keyboard for a moment. "That night at the club, when Loren gave you our numbers, she stepped outside and called me immediately before she did it. Unfortunately, by the time I got my ass in gear and got moving to get over to the club, you two had already left. Loren said that when she went to go into the bathroom, Jack had stepped forward to stop her and she told him if he didn't get the fuck out of her way, he'd wish he had."

Betsy's heart thumped. "I didn't know."

"I'm sure he didn't tell you. But Loren said it wasn't long after that he hustled you out of there."

That was exactly what had happened. At the time, Betsy hadn't known why. He'd asked her if Loren had said anything to her while she was in the bathroom, and she'd flat-out lied and said she'd heard someone come in and wash their hands, but hadn't spoken to them.

All the while, thinking about the slip of paper hiding in her bra. She hadn't had her purse with her. Jack had put her license in his wallet for the evening. He'd asked to see her hands when she'd walked out, and she thanked god she'd thought to hide the paper.

When she'd stripped upon returning to the apartment, yes, Jack had paid more attention than usual, and then his demeanor changed, going back to normal once she was naked.

She'd quickly let that incident slip from her mind. Mostly so she didn't risk him thinking something had happened once he'd appeared satisfied that it hadn't.

"So," Tilly said, "when you start thinking you have this huge burden of guilt for what's happening now, dump it. There are several of us shouldering our own burdens of guilt that you're in this position. No, we can't police everyone. We're not a nanny state, for chrissake. People are adults and we can't stop every bad decision out there. But several of us comparing notes realized too late, unfortunately, that we should have stepped in sooner. If nothing else, to get you alone, speak with you, and make sure you were okay. And we failed you as friends. And for that, *we* feel guilty."

She'd had no idea. Betsy had assumed she was totally alone now. Well, before Saturday night. She'd assumed once Jack had cut her parents out of the picture that it was her against...well, everyone. Because Jack had sworn that if she tried to leave him, he'd ruin her, turn any- and everyone against her.

Then Loren had slipped her their phone numbers.

Never would she have dreamed that maybe everyone was already against *him*.

"This is how today will go," Tilly said. "Finish eating. I'm going to make sure I can print something and access the Internet before they leave. We're going to get you a shower and get you dressed and then we're going to go see Ted Collins at his office to talk to him for a little while. I'm also taking you shopping. Back here, work on your resume, and then comes the hard part."

That *all* sounded hard right at that moment. "The hard part?"

She looked grim. "We're going to track down your parents, and you're going to let me talk to them."

Cold fear filled her. "My parents?"

Tilly set her laptop on the coffee table and turned to her. "You haven't actually talked to your parents, have you?"

She shook her head.

"When and what was your last contact with them?"

"I sent them a Christmas card, but that was before Jack talked to them that night."

"You mean the phone call you aren't even sure really happened?"

"But I was right there when he called them!"

"He called someone, but you don't know who. He could have called his own fucking voicemail, for all you know. Or he could have faked making a call."

Betsy wasn't sure if her thrumming pulse was from fear or hope.

"Maybe he did call them," Tilly continued. "Maybe he called them and sent them pictures. Maybe he didn't. But do you want to spend the rest of your life not knowing for sure?"

She shook her head. "No," she whispered.

"Did they ever send you any mail?"

"No. I sent them my new address, too."

"Sent them how?"

"I mailed them a card."

"*You* mailed them a card?"

"Yeah, I gave…" Her voice trailed off.

Tilly grimly nodded. "You gave it to him and he supposedly mailed it for you."

Heat filled her face. She nodded.

"Right. Here's what I'm going to hope is the best-case scenario. That we contact your parents today and they are overjoyed to hear from their missing daughter, whom they were worried might have fallen off the face of the damned planet. Second-best-case is that Jack told them you didn't want anything to do with them and they let it go. Worst-case is he did send them pictures and talked to them. But somehow, I doubt he did that."

"Why?"

"Because he would have been risking your parents calling the cops to do a welfare check. I know if I had a daughter and some douche called me and told me what Jack supposedly told your parents, as soon as I hung up the goddamned phone, I'd be calling the cops to go check on her."

"Oh."

Tilly cocked her head. "What?"

It took her a moment to answer. "I felt really hurt by them just accepting what he said and did without wanting to talk to me about it."

"You did, huh?"

"Yeah. He even made a point of twisting it around. Saying that he could accept me as 'freaky' but they couldn't. Meaning he was right to take control over me because I didn't belong with 'vanillas.'"

And then he'd followed it with a tender session to "prove" to her that he loved her.

Betsy felt ludicrous admitting all of that now, but in the cold light of day, and in the safety of Kenny and Nolan's living room, and with Tilly's strong shoulder to lean on, she realized how deep she'd been dragged into Jack's bullshit at the time.

"And you never, at the time, thought he might be pulling one over on you?" Tilly gently asked.

Her left eye blurred with tears as she slowly shook her head. "How fucking stupid am I?"

Tilly hugged her. "Okay, another rule. Stop saying *that*. You're *not* stupid. You made a bad choice about who to trust. Believe me, we've all done that at least once in our lives. Eat your breakfast, and we'll get through today. Hopefully by tonight you'll have at least one emotional boulder rolled off your back."

Chapter Ten

Luckily, Tilly hadn't come armed with only her laptop. Before the guys left, Tilly went out to her SUV and brought in a shower chair. "This was Lan's. I loaned it to Abbey after her back surgery because she wasn't supposed to bend over." She smiled. "Hopefully you won't need it for long, but trust me, it's your new best friend."

After the men left for work, Tilly helped Betsy into the shower. Yes, the shower chair proved to be a godsend. Tilly made Betsy do some slow, careful stretching under the warm water, while Tilly held the shower head for her. Then she made Betsy shave what she could reach of her legs before Tilly helped to finish what she couldn't.

"Feeling better?" Tilly asked as she combed out Betsy's hair.

"Lots."

Betsy forced herself to stare into the mirror at her reflection. Her face looked horrible still, some of the bruises already starting to transform from purple to an ugly brownish green that was almost worse. Her right eye was a little less swollen today than it had been, but it still looked horrific.

In the bedroom, Tilly started dumping bags of clothes that the men had grabbed from the apartment—what few there were—onto the bed and sorting them. The dresser drawers in the guest bedroom were empty, as was the closet. So Tilly started folding and putting them away.

"I'm noticing a distinct lack of any kind of professional clothes," Tilly noted. "And remind me to give extra kudos to Kenny for what he picked out for you. Dude has style. Let me guess, Jack made you get rid of your work clothes?"

"Yeah," Betsy admitted. Tilly had helped her dress in the comfortable jersey maxi skirt and a different loose top. They were some of the very few clothes Jack had allowed her to keep that weren't fetish gear.

"Okay, seriously, what the hell?" Tilly asked as she finished putting everything away. "You've got like less than a week's worth of regular clothes."

"He wouldn't let me wear clothes at home unless it was cold," she said.

"Oh." Tilly's mouth pressed into a grim line. "I know some people do that, but they usually have exemptions for daily stuff. And they don't throw away the rest of someone's clothes in the process."

"He decided what he thought I needed and I had to donate the rest to Goodwill."

"Okay." She sat on the edge of the bed next to Betsy and took her hands in hers. "Do you trust me?"

Betsy nodded. Tilly was one of the few people in this world whom she absolutely trusted.

"Will you *please* indulge me for at least the next few days?"

"What do you mean?"

She gently tucked Betsy's damp hair back behind her ears. "I am not going to be able to be around much for you over the next several months once I start working for Leigh, Lucas, and Nick. So I want to do as much as I can, right *now*, while I can. June, Loren, and Eliza will step in as your primary mentors once I'm out of town, but I called dibs on getting the ball rolling.

"I have what most people would probably label an enchanted life, if they didn't know my history. Which, quite honestly, isn't something I'm going to burden you with today. Let's just say I earned my good fortune. And I have a very rich husband. I also have no sisters or nieces or daughters, and never will. All I have are friends I've adopted as family. Meaning when I want to spoil them, I do."

She gently took Betsy's hands in hers. "Saturday was a symbolic birthday for you. A *re*birthday. And I want, as your friend and someone who cares about you, to spoil you rotten over it. Can you *please* let me do that, without you feeling guilty about it? I wouldn't be doing this if I couldn't afford it. I will also admit it will help me assuage at least a little of my own guilt about what happened. All right?"

Betsy nodded. "Thank you." She leaned in and hugged her. "Thank you guys for saving me."

It was comforting to feel Tilly's arms around her, holding her, stroking her back. It'd been a long time since she'd felt that kind of true safety and love.

"You can thank all of us by showing us the kick-ass woman I know you are, rising above this, and making us all proud."

"I promise."

"Good. Now, another question. How long's it been since you've been to the hair salon?"

Betsy shook her head. "Since I moved in with Jack. Months. He wanted me to grow it out long."

"How do *you* want it to look?"

"I...I don't know anymore."

"Well, we also have an appointment at my hair stylist. I bribed her to come in today. So we need to get you ready."

"I can't go out like this." The last thing she wanted—the last thing she could emotionally handle at that time—was a salon full of nosy women staring at her.

"Yes, you can. She's normally closed on Mondays. It'll just be us. Wait here." She left the room and returned with the tote bag. In it, a brand new, large, floppy-brimmed hat, large sunglasses, and some makeup.

"I wasn't exactly sure of your skin tone, so I made my best guess. But honestly, that doesn't matter. I was more worried about the concealer. Hold still."

Tilly opened the new containers of cosmetics and gently started applying concealer, foundation, and powder to Betsy's face and neck, being careful around her stitches and swollen eye.

Fifteen minutes later, she sat back and tipped her head as she examined her handiwork. "Put the glasses on."

The new sunglasses still had the tag on them. Tilly reached over and ripped the tag off and handed them to her.

"Better. They hide the stitches and the worst of your eye. It's obvious there's something off, but let's try the hat."

Tilly removed the tag and handed it to her. Betsy donned it, then Tilly made a couple of slight adjustments to the hat before smiling.

"There. You look like a movie star going incognito." She helped Betsy stand and made her look at herself in the mirror over the dresser.

Yes, there was a glimmer of who she used to be staring back at her, but the person in the mirror was still a stranger.

"Thank you for this," Betsy said.

Tilly snorted. "Thank my husband's black AmEx," she said. "Girlfriend, we *are* going shopping later."

* * * *

The hair stylist was nice, chatty, and pretended there was absolutely nothing at all wrong with Betsy's face. She guessed Tilly must have warned her about how bad she'd look, or the stylist was lethal at poker.

Either way, two hours later, Betsy had her first haircut in the better part of a year, layered and hanging at her shoulders, where she'd used to wear it. The stylist had *tsked* at the poor condition of her hair due to no conditioner and the cheap shampoo Jack had forced her to use, and started off with doing a hot oil treatment that left it feeling better than it had in…well, a long damn time.

She also colored it, adding a few highlights to it and removing the grey starting to creep in, which made a huge difference and made Betsy look younger. Tilly asked the stylist to load them up with product Betsy would need and to add it to the tab.

Once Tilly helped Betsy touch up her makeup and put the hat and glasses back into place, she paid the bill and thanked the stylist with a long hug and a whispered something before taking Betsy's hand and leading her out to her SUV.

"Where to now?" Betsy asked.

"Ted's. We're going to eat lunch there at his office while you chat. I can sit in with you, if you'd like, or I can wait outside."

"With me, please."

"No problem. I brought ibuprofen, too, for your pain. I'm sure you're close to needing some."

The pain wasn't quite as debilitating as it had been, but yes, it still hurt. "Thank you." Her right foot and ankle ached, but Tilly had examined her wounds and determined they weren't infected.

Ted welcomed them with smiles and an especially gentle hug for Betsy before leading them into his office and closing the door. Tilly and Betsy settled together on the sofa. Betsy took her hat and sunglasses off and set them on the arm of the sofa.

"I'm going to order us pizza, if that's okay?" Ted asked.

Betsy nodded.

Ted cocked his head. "Betsy?"

"It's fine."

She didn't miss how he and Tilly exchanged a glance. "I'm fine with pizza, honestly. If there's something I don't like, I'll pick it off."

Tilly's hand shot up like a kid in class. "Oooh, me! Pick me!"

Ted rolled his eyes, but waved a hand at Tilly to speak.

She turned and leaned forward toward Betsy. "Honey, this isn't a dictatorship. If you don't like pizza, or don't want pizza, or specifically don't want something on your pizza, say so."

How long had it been before now since she'd *had* a choice? "Do they make a white sauce pizza?" she timidly asked, hating the way her voice sounded.

"They do," Ted said. "A very good one. Would you prefer white sauce?"

She nodded. "Please. And I like mushrooms."

"Sounds good to me. We have sodas, water, and tea, or coffee, here at the office. Is that all right?"

Betsy nodded.

"Good. Let me get it ordered and we'll get started."

Tilly reached over and patted her on the leg. "See? That was easy. Baby steps."

Betsy thought about her sore right ankle. "It's about the only kind I can take right now."

* * * *

Betsy had never seen a counsellor before, had no experience with the process whatsoever. She wasn't even sure what to expect and sat there nervously picking at her cuticles while Ted ordered the pizza.

With that done, Ted surprised her by starting with one simple question.

"Where do you see yourself in one year?"

She looked up when she realized he was talking to her. "Me?"

He nodded. "You."

A flurry of flippant lines crossed through her brain but she caught herself. Jack had hated her one-liners, her quips, her comebacks.

She'd been backhanded plenty of times when she'd said something without thinking about it. Things others had always laughed over. She loved making people laugh.

With Jack, she'd learned to stay quiet.

"I don't know," she admitted.

Ted didn't say anything. He simply looked at her as if expecting her to continue.

"I *really* don't know," she said.

He arched an eyebrow but didn't speak. Even Tilly remained uncharacteristically silent next to her.

Betsy thought about it and finally said the first thing that came to mind. "A year ago, if you'd told me I'd be sitting right *here*, under *these* circumstances, I would have said you were nuts. That I'd let a guy do *this* to me? No flipping way."

"Were you involved in BDSM a year ago?" Ted asked.

"I'd just started, yeah. Had been to a few munches. A couple of classes. I knew this was what I wanted. Not *this*, obviously. But BDSM. I wanted a loving Dominant who'd respect my boundaries and make me feel safe."

"Why?"

She blinked, staring at him. "Why what?"

"Any of that. Why?"

"I don't know."

He leveled his gaze at her. Now she felt a little of his Dom stepping out of the shadows and into view. She suspected this wasn't something that normally happened with his other clients.

"Look me in the eyes," he said, "and as soon as I finish asking the question, you immediately answer me with the first thing that comes to mind without censoring yourself or thinking about it, okay?"

She nodded.

He crossed his arms in front of him on his desk and leaned forward a little.

Yes, definitely Dom-tude in his gaze.

"*Why* did you want a loving Dominant who would respect your boundaries and make you feel safe?"

The answer welled up from inside her, beyond her control. "Because for once I wanted someone I could trust and lean on and not feel alone, and feel like I finally belonged somewhere," she whispered before bursting into tears.

* * * *

Ted handed Tilly the box of tissues before stepping out with the excuse of getting their drinks.

Tilly immediately ripped a handful from the box and pressed them into Betsy's hands before wrapping her arms around Betsy and letting her sob.

"You're not alone," Tilly whispered. "Sweetie, you're *not* alone. You have all of us. I know it's not the same, but it's a start. Just don't close us out."

"Tilly, I fucked up sooo bad," she whispered, barely able to speak. "Look what I did to my life. How am I ever supposed to trust any guy ever again after what I did? I should have said stop so many times and I didn't."

"Are you religious?"

"Not really. I went to church when I was a kid. Why?"

"You know the difference between a cult and a religion, right?"

"Yeah?"

"Do you know there's that one that's in Clearwater? That famous one. There are people who spent decades of their lives, I'm talking people high up in that so-called 'church,' who devoted everything to it, just to quit. And by quitting, they lost everything, including friends, family, kids, sometimes spouses. And sometimes, they fought tooth and nail to stay in before they finally quit."

"Why?"

"Because they finally realized it was harmful for them to be in it, for whatever reason. There are people who escape cults every *day* because they realize it's harmful for them. But does that make other religions bad?"

"No."

"Exactly. Does that make the people who got out of those cults wrong or bad people?"

"No."

"Exactly. Are you old enough to remember hearing about that crazy fucker in South America who killed himself and his followers by ordering they drink poisoned Kool-Aid?"

"Yeah?"

"*That's* earth-shattering. That's *bad.* Honey, this is painful, yes. It takes, what, nine months to grow a baby. Based on what you've told me already, you were ready to leave Jack a while ago, weren't you?"

"Yeah."

"I'm going to borrow a trick from Ted's book. No thinking, just answer me this—what kept you with Jack?"

"Fear," she said without having to think about it. She blew her nose.

"Okay. So let's say nine months, ballpark then. You grew a baby. Your life changed. The baby, instead of being a pooping and peeing and crying and barfing little brick of joy turned out to be a nine-pound bundle of self-realization and experience. Right?"

"I guess."

Ted returned with their drinks, handing cold bottles of water to Tilly and Betsy and taking his cold bottle of Mountain Dew to his desk.

"How are you doing?" he asked Betsy.

"I quit drinking the Kool-Aid before it killed me," she quietly said.

He looked puzzled. "I'm sorry, I thought you asked for water?"

Tilly fell over laughing.

* * * *

With the pizza delivered and served and Ted brought up to speed, this time he let Betsy talk, leading her through what had happened, from meeting Jack until finally making the break on Saturday.

It took an hour and a box of tissues, but Betsy felt a lot lighter when they finished talking. She didn't feel any less angry at herself for being so gullible, but she had to admit now she had a starting point to work from going forward. She had things to do. She had goals to make, focus to find, and dreams to define.

She started feeling the beginnings of *her* returning.

Ted was still trying to get in touch with his friends about taking her on as a client. But meanwhile, he wanted to see her back there on Thursday at ten, an appointment Tilly assured him would be kept, even if someone else had to bring her.

Tilly went with her to the restroom to help her wash her face and reapply the concealer and powder. With the hat and glasses back in position, her disguise was once more complete.

"How's this?" Betsy asked her.

Tilly hugged her. "I think in a couple of weeks you'll look almost normal again and maybe even start feeling that way a little."

She drove Betsy to the mall close to Nolan and Kenny's house. Tilly started them at an Old Navy for some basics for Betsy, including shorts, slacks, jeans, a couple of casual sundresses, and blouses. Then Tilly, who wouldn't let Betsy carry the bags, led her to a high-end department store, where Tilly started finding business clothes for her, then some nice bras and panties.

Betsy knew arguing would be pointless, so despite feeling guilty that her friend was spending the money on her, Betsy didn't fight her, tried on everything Tilly shoved at her, spoke up when there was a color or style she didn't really like…and said thank you.

A lot.

Tilly finished off the shopping trip at a shoe store, where she got Betsy three pairs of dressy flats, a pair of loafers, and two pairs of sandals.

“Now,” Tilly said, finally letting her carry a couple of shopping bags as they returned to her SUV, “we’re going to go home, you’re going to change from what you’re wearing into one of the outfits I just bought you, and we’re going work on your resume.”

“Why do I need to change?”

“You’re going to dress the part to get the part.”

“I should call the office I worked for, too.”

“We’ll do that first. *After* you change clothes.”

“Yes, Ma’am.”

Tilly smiled. “Well, I’m not your Domme, but I’ll let you call me that. I’d rather you do that if it makes you feel better.”

“Thanks.”

“Hey, that’s what friends are for, sweetie.” Her smile faded as she started the car. “Believe me, I wouldn’t be here talking to you right now if it wasn’t for friends.”

Chapter Eleven

While Betsy used the bathroom, Tilly laid an outfit out on the bed, including shoes. Betsy washed her hands and stared at her reflection in the mirror. Taking off the sunglasses and hat, she looked at the swollen shape of her right eye under the concealer. The bruising still painfully evident despite Tilly's best efforts. The stitches, of course, still there.

But…

The hair. No, she hadn't had it professionally colored when she was getting it cut. Sometimes she bought store color and did it when she noticed grey, but she had to admit she liked the look. It felt lighter, healthier, had shine and bounce and a little natural curl that had been missing for months as it grew longer, stragglier at the ends despite her trying to trim the dead ends herself when Jack wasn't home to see her do it.

It was her hair.

Hers.

She reached up and fluffed it with her fingers in a way she hadn't been able to do in months.

Familiar.

She fluffed it again, carefully shaking her head just a little, not enough to jostle her still-sore muscles.

The hint of a smile curved her lips. It did look good. It looked freaking amazing.

She went to the bedroom and Tilly helped her change clothes. Tilly let her leave off the bra, knowing she was still too sore to tolerate wearing it, but the slacks, blouse, blazer, and flats made her feel…

Normal.

She turned and looked in the mirror there as Tilly stood next to her. "That's a pretty good-looking woman right there," Tilly said to her reflection. "Wait until your outer bruises are healed up, and you're going to be a knock-out." Tilly winced. "Bad choice of words, sorry."

That made Betsy smile, even though it hurt.

"You know what I see?" Tilly asked.

"What?"

"I see a woman reborn. Stronger, tougher, harder. In the good ways. Scarred in the painful ways, yeah. But that scarring will eventually let you take chances later on, safe chances, that will make you happy. Like calluses on your feet."

"You think so?"

"Honey, been there, done that, got the T-shirt. I know where the landmines are because I laid those fuckers with my own two hands."

She turned to Betsy. "No, I can't do the work for you. And no, my situation wasn't exactly like yours. In some ways, mine was better, and in some ways, mine was worse. Doesn't matter. But trust us to lead you through those damn landmines. We won't carry you, but just keep up, walking with us, and we'll get you safely through to the other side no matter how scary it feels at times. Deal?"

"Deal."

Fortunately, the expected disappointment of her first phone call didn't knock Betsy totally off her feet emotionally. Yes, obviously, her position had been filled. And no, unless Betsy had a real estate license, they didn't have any other positions. But the agency's owner did tell Betsy to list her as a reference in her job hunt, and asked for her e-mail address so she could send Betsy a letter of recommendation she could use in her job search.

Tilly counted that as a win, and Betsy couldn't argue with her.

Then Tilly got her computer booted up again, pulled up a resume template in Word, and handed the machine over to Betsy.

It felt…weird to be holding a laptop again, even though…before…she'd spent hours on one at work, or sitting on her sofa in her small apartment in front of the TV at night doing stuff on one.

"What do I do?" she asked Tilly.

"Fill the stuff in where it says. I won't do it for you. If your fingers were broken, yeah. No offense, my love is of the tough kind, believe it or not." She pointed at the laptop. "Get busy."

Twenty minutes later, Tilly was reading over her shoulder and proofreading a printed copy of it. "That looks good. I'll e-mail the file to you, along with Shayla's e-mail address."

"Why hers?"

"She's a writer. You are going to text her and ask if she'll proofread it for you."

"I don't want to impo—"

Tilly glared at her as she held up a finger, silencing her. "What did I just say?" she quietly asked.

"To text Shayla and ask her to proofread it."

"Did I ask you to question me?"

"No, Ma'am."

Tilly's face broke into a beaming smile and she threw her arms around Betsy as she laughed. "Okay, seriously, save that only for fun. Learn to stop questioning your friends when we say something. If I thought it would be an imposition, I wouldn't have told you to do it. Shayla already passed along to me that she would help you if you needed it. Okay? That was a test. And yes, you failed, but hopefully you'll learn to trust us."

"I do trust you guys."

"Then trust us when we say we want to help you. All right? Or get back into the healthy habit of not being afraid to ask. Asking is not a bad thing. You might get a yes, or you might get a no, but you'll never get an answer if you don't ask. Right?"

"Right."

"Now text Shayla and ask her."

Betsy reached for her phone. In less than two minutes, Shayla had texted back that she'd be waiting to receive it and get to work on it for her immediately.

Somehow, Betsy managed to blink back her tears over that reply and e-mailed the document to Shayla from her phone, where Betsy had created a new e-mail account.

Tilly smiled and held up her fist.

Betsy fist-bumped her back.

"And now, for the next part."

"What's that?"

Tilly's smile faded as she pointed at Betsy's phone.

* * * *

Apparently, even Tilly knew the limits of Betsy's endurance. She told Betsy to plug her mom's cell number into the phone but not hit send, that she would make the first contact. Fortunately, Betsy knew the number by heart.

She hoped it was still a good number, because her parents didn't have a landline since they'd moved up north. They hadn't needed one.

Betsy's hand trembled as she handed the phone over.

"What's her name?" Tilly asked.

"Karen. Karen Lambert."

Tilly took a deep breath and crossed her fingers before punching the speaker option button and then hitting send.

In the quiet of the house, Betsy could clearly hear the phone ringing on the other end as the call connected. After three rings, Betsy was sure that it would go to voice mail, but then a cautious woman's voice answered.

"Hello?"

Betsy choked back a relieved sob that it sounded like her mom. Tilly took over. "Hello, my name is Tilly Cardinal-LaCroux, and I'm calling from Sarasota, Florida. I'm trying to reach Karen Lambert on behalf of her daughter, Betsy Lambert."

There was a long pause. Betsy closed her eyes, afraid—no, certain—that her mom was going to hang up.

Then, "Is she all right? Please, tell me, is she okay? Is she alive?"

Tilly took the call off speaker mode, stood, and as she spoke quickly headed down the hallway and into the men's bedroom office where she closed the door behind her.

Stunned, Betsy sat there quivering, terrified, unable to process. She both did and didn't want to know came next, wanted and didn't want to hear what Tilly said.

She felt like a faker sitting there in her pricey, new business suit and good shoes—better than she could have bought before on her salary—and the concealer caked across the injuries on her face. She wrapped her arms around herself and somehow managed not to cry as she waited.

And waited.

And waited.

Twenty minutes later, she heard Tilly's voice as the office door opened and then she walked down the hall, still talking.

"Yes, here she is."

Then Tilly was standing in front of her, the phone held out to her in one hand, and a box of tissues in the other.

When Betsy looked up, she realized Tilly had been crying.

Correction, was *still* crying.

Tilly shook the phone at her.

Betsy finally reached out and took it, choking back fear and regret and dread as she forced the word out. "Mom?"

It sounded like her mom had already been crying, but she loudly sobbed when she heard Betsy's voice. "Bets? Is that really you, baby?

Oh, my god, we were afraid you were dead. We love you so, so much."

"I love you, too, Mom."

* * * *

Betsy talked—cried—to her mom for so long that Tilly had to go get the phone charger from Betsy's bedroom and find an extension cord so she could plug it in and not make her move from where she was on the couch. During that time, her father had arrived home from work and she tearfully got to talk to him, too. It was after six thirty when she finally got off the phone with them minutes before Kenny arrived home to find Betsy and Tilly on the couch, crying in each other's arms.

"Oh, my god! What's wrong?" He ran over, with such a look of horrified terror on his face that it started both of them giggling, then laughing.

"He never called my parents," Betsy finally managed. "The son of a bitch never even *talked* to them. They had no idea who he was until Tilly told my mom what happened."

He pulled up, looking confused, which made them both laugh even harder.

He closed his eyes, as if thinking for a moment. "Oookaaay, I'm going to play the stupid guy card here and guess you're laughing at me for freaking out just now, right?"

They giggled, nodding.

"Aaannd you were crying when I came in because you were…happy?"

"Relieved," the women said in unison, which started even more giggling between them.

Betsy couldn't remember the last time she giggled.

Giggled!

And she'd never seen Tilly cry before, so she knew that had to be a massively earth-shaking thing she'd think about later on when she could actually process coherent thoughts again.

Tilly took a few deep breaths, stood, and hugged Kenny. Then she wiped at her face and took one more deep breath as she pointed a finger at him.

"You tell anyone you saw me crying, you're singing soprano the hard way. Got it?"

He nodded, which made Betsy giggle yet again.

Tilly patted him on the shoulder and headed back down the hall. A moment later, they heard the bathroom door shut.

Kenny sank to the couch next to her. "You look…wow. Did she take you to get your hair done?"

"Yeah." She fought queasy nerves. "Do you like it?"

"I…the question is, do *you* like it?"

She nodded.

"Honestly? You look, well, obviously, besides…" He sort of pointed at her face with one hand and zigzagged his index finger around. "Your hair looks amazing! You look a lot more…peaceful now. Which is a weird comment to go with a hair compliment, I know, but you do."

"Thank you," she said, remembering Tilly's lecture.

"And the outfit is great, too."

"More Tilly." She laid the phone on the coffee table and turned to him. "Thank you for everything you and Nolan have done for me. Thank you for the phone, and thank you for your kindness and hospitality. I really, really appreciate it."

* * * *

Kenny sensed something drastically different about this woman sitting before him, and not even her hair or her clothes.

"You're very welcome," he said. "What's going on?"

"She took me to talk to Ted," Betsy said. "And I'm going back on Thursday to talk to him. And we obviously did hair and shopping. And she made me type up my resume, and text Shayla to ask to send it to her. And then she talked to my mom. Then I got to talk to my mom and my dad."

He didn't interrupt her, sensing she was working her way up to something big.

"I want you to be honest with me while I'm here," she said. "If I get to be a pain or a burden, please be honest with me. Tilly has driven the point home that I'm not alone. I *know* there are other people who will help me out. But I want to rebuild my friendships and make new ones, and if me staying here at any time tests or strains my friendship with you and Nolan, I would rather move out than lose this friendship. I know we don't know each other very well yet, but I'd like to. And I don't want to do something stupid and risk any friendships. I want you to call me out if you think I'm wrong about something. I want you to hold me accountable."

It took him a moment once she finished talking to finally come up with a response. The quiet, earnest frankness of her words had blown him away.

"Thanks. We will. I don't want to jeopardize our friendship, either."

Now she looked exhausted, worn, as if she'd been strong too long and she'd hit a wall. "I'm sorry I'm not helping cook dinner tonight."

"It's okay. Nolan's stopping by Publix and grabbing a chicken dinner from the deli. No cooking."

Tilly returned from the bathroom, her face now washed and free of makeup. But her eyes still looked a little puffy, her nose red.

"Okay. Well, this was a productive day." She gathered up her laptop and then hugged Betsy. "I'll be back in the morning, same time. I believe June will be here on Wednesday, but I'll confirm that with her for sure, and probably Loren on Thursday."

Tilly smacked herself in the forehead. "Yoga clothes. June said you can come to her classes for free right now. I should have bought you some yoga clothes."

"I got her a couple of pairs of yoga pants," Kenny said.

"Perfect!"

Before Kenny could get Tilly to expand upon that, she was saying good-bye and blowing out the door, laptop case over her shoulder.

Kenny stared at the front door for a moment in confusion, then looked at Betsy. "Wow."

Betsy smiled, and for the first time since Saturday night, it looked real, not forced. "Wow is right. In the good ways."

* * * *

In the back of Betsy's mind, however, she still harbored a lot of anxiety over what potential landmines still lurked out there. Tony stopped by later that evening to return her laptop after Nolan had come home and they'd already eaten dinner.

Tony and another friend, Mike, had thoroughly gone over the machine, combed through all of Jack's online accounts, and deleted every shred of evidence Jack had on her that they could find. Pictures, e-mails, anything that remotely had to do with her. They printed out damning information that outlined some of his plans for her and getting her under his control. Then they went in, after screen-capping everything, and either deleted the accounts or changed the passwords, secret questions, and contact information so there was no way Jack could gain control of them again. Tony and Mike now had full control of them.

The only things they left intact were Jack's bank account, his cellphone account, and his utilities accounts.

Not that Jack would be able to pay his bills anyway while sitting in jail.

And they'd deleted his primary e-mail account as well, so he wouldn't be able to use it to log back into those accounts unless he remembered his passwords to them.

Betsy wouldn't let the fact that Jack had taken the computer and used it—a computer she'd originally bought with her own money before meeting him—deter her from using it now. Tony had wiped Jack's presence from it and restored it to a date just before she'd handed it over to Jack.

It was like he'd never had his slimy hands on it in the first place.

And, lucky for her, Jack had not deleted her e-mail account like she'd thought he had. He'd only changed the password, which Tony had been able to retrieve since Jack had set his e-mail address as the backup. Tony reset it, as well as her Facebook and Twitter accounts.

Tony showed her how to add the new Gmail account she'd created on her phone to her existing Gmail account, so she could receive those e-mails in the same account, as well as get her old Gmail e-mails on her phone.

It felt like a chunk of *her* had been restored. A chunk of her that Jack had desperately tried to erase in his attempts to completely own her.

"Can I set up a new FetLife account?" she asked. They'd found hers, deactivated by Jack, and reactivated it for her.

They'd changed Jack's account, not wanting to deactivate it yet until they'd gone through and screencapped all the evidence of his contacts with other submissives, both in Florida and in Michigan. Tony and Ross wanted to contact the people to let them know about Jack's arrest in case they had stories of their own they wanted to tell.

Or perhaps charges they wanted to file.

And they delinked him from her relationship-wise, and her from him.

They'd also found out he'd been actively talking to two other subs on FetLife within the past few weeks, messages that indicated he might have been trying to groom them to be his next slaves despite having Betsy chained in his apartment.

Tony had written to them from his own account, with the conversations copied and pasted into his messages to them, so they knew he wasn't just faking when he warned them off Jack and about the close brush they'd had with an abusive asshat.

"That's up to you," Tony said. "I suggest only friending people you actually know in person. I also suggest sending people private messages when you friend them, to tell them who you are and why your new identity needs to be kept secret. I definitely would not use your old account. I would change the screen name and hold onto it, if you wanted, but the URL and user number doesn't change if you do that. Use the new one for your new activity just in case Jack has a way of finding out your old one."

She looked to Nolan and Kenny. "What do you think?"

Kenny held up his hands. "That's up to you."

"I miss being able to keep in touch with my friends," she said.

"I don't blame you," Nolan replied.

She thought about it. "Obviously, no face pics."

Tony smiled. "To quote Tilly, *duh*."

"I can say I'm in Tampa or something, not Sarasota."

"Again, that's wise," Tony said. "Or, I hear there's a massive kinky population in Antarctica these days." He smiled.

Chapter Twelve

Tuesday morning, after the men left for work, Tilly got Betsy up and moving and into the shower, where Betsy was actually able to shave more of her legs by herself before asking for Tilly's help.

Tilly made her get dressed in the same outfit she'd worn the afternoon before, since it'd only been worn for a couple of hours. Then they sat at the dining room table in front of Betsy's laptop and started her online job search.

Plus Betsy e-mailed her resume, and the letter of recommendation from her former employer, to Kenny's mom.

By lunchtime, Betsy had to admit despite physically feeling like crap, mentally it felt like she'd tipped her head sideways and a literal ton of cobwebs and dust and debris had fallen out her ear, leaving nothing behind in her skull but a clean, blank slate.

She also knew that feeling likely wouldn't last. Ted had warned her to be ready for mood swings.

Tilly had also come by with another present, a Kindle, on which she'd purchased and downloaded over a dozen books Ted had recommended Betsy read to help her on her recovery journey.

So now she had homework, in addition to her job search.

And she was now texting back and forth with her mother and father. Which was a miracle in and of itself, since her father wasn't big on texting. They had wanted to pay to fly her up to visit them, but Betsy didn't want to do that yet. It would be too easy to let them talk her into moving in with them and staying and letting them take care of her.

That was something she knew she couldn't do. Visiting them would have to wait until she was strong enough to take care of herself. Her life—what was left of it—was here in Florida. She didn't want to leave Florida. She was reconnecting with friends here now, and didn't want to derail that fragile, tenuous progress.

Tilly driving, they met Loren and Eliza for lunch. Betsy still had the sunglasses and hat, but today she'd tried applying the makeup herself and managed it without too many problems.

She felt somewhat self-conscious, but having her friends there to talk to made a huge difference and allowed her not to worry about if anyone was looking at her and wondering if she had been beaten up.

"Tomorrow," Tilly said, "June will be there. I have to meet with Leigh about going out to LA. I can't put that off any longer. But you're going to be in good hands."

"And you have me on Thursday," Eliza said.

"And me on Friday," Loren volunteered.

"Saturday and Sunday," Tilly added, "the guys have said they'll be home with you all day, so no worries there. Next week, Eliza will take over arranging the schedule. You can text and call me anytime. Unless I'm on a plane, in which case I'll get back to you as soon as I can."

"I won't let you down," Betsy swore. "I'm going to work my ass off and get back on my feet. I promise."

"That's all we ask," Tilly said. "Because we want to see you succeed."

* * * *

On Wednesday, June arrived before the men left for work. Betsy didn't know her very well, but knew she was a trusted friend of the others.

That meant, by default, June already had Betsy's trust.

Betsy was done trying to figure out who to trust and who not to trust. There was a clearly delineated circle of friends in the Suncoast Society munch group who knew and trusted each other. That was good enough for her. If someone wasn't well-established within that strict circle, Betsy would give them a wide berth, no matter now nice and friendly they seemed.

Hell, at this point, she was ready to give Tilly and Eliza full control over her selections in play and romantic partners for the rest of her life. She'd obviously failed miserably—dangerously so—at her first attempt to enter the BDSM dating pool. Yes, she'd done okay playing, but when crossing the boundary from play to having more she'd once again screwed up.

The next time could kill her if she messed it up as badly as she had this time. Hell, she was probably lucky she wasn't dead.

At least now she had her parents back in her life. More guilt there, that they'd been so worried about her all these months. There was relief that Jack had not talked to them at all.

But it left a bad taste in Betsy's throat that she'd had to admit to her parents there was a possibility Jack might one day send pictures of her to them. She didn't go into detail, and they didn't ask, but they made it clear that if it happened, they'd simply report him to the cops for it.

And they wouldn't love her any less for it, either.

After June helped her with her shower, she had Betsy dress in the yoga pants, sneakers, and a tanktop and they headed south.

"Where are we going?" Betsy asked.

June smiled. "Mental health day."

Betsy recognized the turnoff for the northern road to Manasota Key. June bypassed the northern public beach and stopped at the middle one, called Blind Pass Beach, which was nearly deserted.

"Come on." She grabbed two yoga mats from her trunk and led the way across the road from the parking lot to the boardwalk traversing the dunes and down to the sand.

"I don't know yoga," Betsy said as June rolled the mats out onto some firm sand above the high-tide debris line. The water was calm, slow rollers gently lapping at the sand, with only two other people walking along the beach several hundred yards south of them. On a weekday, they had it to themselves.

"We're not doing yoga," she said, adjusting an odd bulge under the right rear side of the waistband of her shorts.

"What's that?" Betsy asked.

June smiled. "Insurance."

Betsy must have looked confused.

"I have a concealed carry permit," June said. "If you think I'm going to stand watch on someone and not carry, think again."

"Does Tilly know that?"

June snorted. "Of course."

June helped Betsy down onto one of the mats. After helping her kick off her sneakers, June took the other mat and sat there, putting her legs into a lotus position.

"I don't expect you to copy me exactly," June said. "Just do what you can." She rested her hands on her knees. "Close your eyes and listen to me. Take a deep breath in and hold it before letting it out…"

Over the next hour, June verbally walked Betsy through a series of guided meditations, of focusing on her emotions, her breathing, the environment around her. The taste of the salty Gulf waters hanging thick in the air, the warmth of the sun on her flesh, the gentle breeze tugging at her hair, which she'd left loose under the hat.

June walked her through recognizing the pain, harnessing it, processing it.

Crying without feeling weaker for it, strengthening her mental and emotional walls without growing hard and cold.

When they finished, June instructed her to perform one final task, to sit and stare at the water, to imagine putting all the negativity she felt about herself on a paper boat and setting it aflame as she shoved it out into the water, to be taken away and absorbed by the waves.

That was what Betsy had completed when her cell phone rang, Ed Payne calling her.

"Hello?"

"Hey, you sitting down?"

Despite the warm afternoon, a chilling dread filled her. "Yeah?"

"He didn't make bail, so it's not that."

Relief washed the dread away. "So what is it?"

"The media's picked up the story," he said. "I've fielded ten calls today from TV and radio stations trying to find you."

The chill returned. "And?"

"Don't worry, they're not finding you. Not through me, at least. But I wanted to warn you before you saw it on the news or someone else told you. Is Tilly there?"

"No, June is."

"Let me speak with her please."

Her good mood shattered, Betsy handed the phone over to June. She spoke with him for a few minutes before ending the call and returning her phone.

"Okay. Well, so much for *that*. I thought you'd get more than a few minutes' of peace out of it."

"No, this was great. Thank you." She stared down at the sand when something caught her eye. Reaching for it, she found a small, black shark's tooth, about the size of the end of her pinky finger.

When she showed June, the woman laughed. "Yeah, we used to bring our girls here all the time looking for them when they were kids. This whole area is known as the shark's teeth capital of the world. You should keep that. Remind you of today. Sharks are always replacing their teeth, you know. They shed them like cats shed fur. That's why they're so efficient."

Betsy stared at it, fingering the tip. "Why's it black?"

"Didn't you ever hunt for them?"

"No."

"The black ones are old. You'll find white ones sometimes, but the black ones are like ancient old. Fossils. Somewhere, a shark was swimming, eating, and lost it. Tens, or maybe hundreds of thousands of years ago. He lost it, or died, and it fell out of his jaw. And now you've found it. Just imagine the odds."

"I thought you said they were common around here?"

"They are, but you found that one. Or it found you. Depends on your point of view. You hungry? I know a great burger place."

They returned home late in the afternoon, but still before the men got home. June helped her rinse off in the shower and change into a pair of PJs. They were just finishing that when Nolan arrived home, laden with grocery bags.

"Can I help?" Betsy asked.

"No," he and June both said together, shooing her into the living room. "Tilly said your assignment tonight is an hour of job hunting, followed by two hours of reading, before you go to bed," June told her.

"Wow. She *is* a sadist," Nolan joked.

* * * *

Nolan walked outside to get another load of groceries, June on his tail. He suspected she wanted to talk about something outside of Betsy's earshot, and she didn't disappoint.

Once she filled him in on the phone call from Ed, Nolan leaned against the side of the car. "Dammit. We knew it was a matter of time, but I was hoping it wouldn't be this soon."

"Since there wasn't a sexual assault," June said, "the media usually won't withhold the name. Ed's been trying to reason with the people and tell them her safety is at risk, but there's another issue, and Ed and I didn't tell her this part."

"What?"

"Jackass has a PD who's trying to file for a bond reduction hearing. If he gets it, and if the judge grants the bond reduction, Jack might be able to make bail."

"Fuck."

"Oh, it gets better. Ed's worried about the possibility of one of the tabloid media outlets trying a side run, maybe offering to foot his bail for an exclusive interview. You know, a BDSM love story gone bad, that kind of bullshit."

He stared at her. "You're kidding, right?"

"I wish I was. It was all I could do not to start ranting about it in front of her. I'll call Tilly and tell her about it, but here's my worry. Jack doesn't know where she is. We've all been passing the word around that no one is to say where she is, even if they know where she is, which of course no one except a few of us do. Emphasize to her tonight, gently and *without* scaring her, that it is vital she does *not* mention where she is or with whom she's staying. To anyone. *Capisce*?"

"Yeah. Why didn't you tell her all this earlier?"

"Because Ed advised me to wait until we got back. He was worried she might get freaked out if she found out while we were out and about. Also, he didn't know if he'd get more information before now. He said he'd call me by now if he had."

She grabbed a couple of grocery bags from the car. "I talked to Laura and Gabe last night. Once Betsy's feeling better, we're going to take her to a gun range in Pt. Charlotte and teach her how to use one. She needs a concealed carry permit."

"Isn't that a little…excessive?"

He knew June and Laura carried. He wasn't sure if Eliza did, but considering Gabe was an FDLE agent, Laura had literally killed a psycho who was trying to kill her, Eliza was a martial arts expert, Brooke was a former archery champion, and Chelbie had fended off a baseball-bat-wielding attacker with only a sex toy and sarcasm, there were some pretty dangerous and deadly women in their own right among their close group of friends.

June stopped and turned, walking back to him. Despite her tiny frame, he felt the urge to lean back, away from her. How Scrye dealt with her, he had no idea, because the fury now visible in the woman's eyes scared the piss out of him.

"No," June calmly and quietly said. "Excessive would be me driving to Tampa and paying cash for a burner cell, having Betsy call him from it to meet her somewhere out in east Manatee County to 'talk,' and then emptying a magazine in his brain pan before I stripped his body, dragged him down to the river, and rolled him into the water, his body weighed down with three concrete blocks, after gutting him so decomposition gas didn't make him float in a few days. *That* would be excessive."

She didn't blink.

Nolan thought he might have pissed himself, just a little.

She widely smiled. "But that would also be illegal, now, wouldn't it?"

He nodded.

"So we're going to teach her how to shoot and defend herself. Legally. Shooting is a great equalizer. Once she's healed, I'm going to start her in my yoga classes to build her flexibility and spirit, and Eliza's going to go with her to ju-whatsits whatever it is she does. Brooke is going to start teaching her archery, which is a completely impractical means of self-defense when compared to fists or a gun in close quarters, but will be a great confidence builder, as well as give her something to focus on. Between all of us, we have a plan. Tilly is our Tyler Durden of protecting Betsy. Only, you know, without blowing shit up."

He stared down at her, leaning back even farther as she leaned in closer. "We all like you and Kenny. We don't have a problem if at some point in the future the three of you hook up. That would be good if it happens in a *healthy* way." Thunderclouds darkened her expression. "But if you guys fuck up, or fuck her over, or fuck *with* her? I'll make Tilly at her meanest look *sweet* by comparison."

Then she smiled, turned, and bounced toward the house with the grocery bags.

He stood there, staring, heart thundering in his chest.

Okay, that time he *definitely* pissed himself a little.

* * * *

Nolan had changed into shorts—and had changed his briefs—and was getting dinner started when Kenny arrived home. Betsy sat on the couch, obediently working on her job search as Tilly had assigned. June had already left.

I guess as long as no one's making soap, we're okay.

Nolan still liked June, but he wouldn't deny she had completely flipped the charts in terms of terrifying. Tilly was now squarely tied for second with Eliza, while June had skyrocketed to number one with a bullet on the scary list.

Literally.

He'd had no doubts in his mind that the woman hadn't just been threatening.

She'd meant every last word.

Kenny walked in, scowling at him as he leaned in to kiss him. "What's wrong?" Kenny asked.

Nolan was about to tell him nothing, almost ashamed to admit he had left a small dribble on the inside of his briefs, which now resided in the dirty clothes hamper, then he remembered the rest of June's news and whispered, "Later."

Kenny went over to say hi to Betsy before he headed back to their bedroom to change. Once Nolan had dinner simmering in the electric skillet, he followed Kenny back to their bedroom, closed the door, and told him what June had told him.

Well, the parts that she said Ed had told her. And about the women banding together to teach Betsy to defend herself.

He left out June's extremely disconcerting asides, because for starters, he wasn't even sure if Kenny would believe him, and secondly, he strongly suspected June wasn't kidding, and he didn't want Kenny to know anything if Jack turned up dead in a river somewhere.

Shot.

Tied to cinder blocks.

And gutted.

The first rule about protecting Betsy is…

When he finished, Kenny looked murderous. Nolan was wondering why he didn't look terrified, except he realized he'd left the terrifying part out.

"That fucker," Kenny muttered as he stripped off his work clothes. "I see that fucker, I'm killing him."

A nervous laugh escaped Nolan. "Yeah, I literally think there'd be a line ahead of you and me, dude."

"I know. Tilly desperately wants a whack at him."

One more nervous burp of laughter he couldn't control. "Yeah, no, not even her."

He remembered once as a kid, not even ten, if that, getting to go to the base with his dad for something. They'd been stationed out in California, and his father was having lunch with some friends. Because it was a Saturday, it was informal, and there'd been some other family function they'd attended that morning.

But what Nolan would never forget were the men he and his father lunched with, men his father had apparently fought with. There'd been a look in some of their eyes as they'd talked, censoring their discussions before they'd gotten to what Nolan at the time had thought of as the "good stuff."

June had a similar expression in her eyes out in their driveway. Cold. Hard.

Deadly.

Tilly was a lot of seriously scary bluster that took care of ninety-nine-point-nine percent of the asshats single female submissives had to deal with in their local group.

June reminded him of a silent, deadly watcher, a ninja.

Waiting.

Then Kenny pulled him in for a kiss, for a moment sidetracking Nolan's brain even to the point of forgetting June's glittering, deadly gaze and that dinner was cooking.

"Yeah. Both of us, together," Kenny said.

"Huh?"

"Killing that guy." Kenny smiled and released Nolan. "I don't know what the future will hold, but I'm glad she came into our lives."

"Yeah. Me, too."

Chapter Thirteen

During dinner, Nolan finally brought the subject up. "June said we need to tell you something," he said. "We didn't want you worrying about it earlier."

There was something disquietingly prey-like in the way her head popped up, eyes wide and nostrils flaring, as if a rabbit preparing to bolt from a predator.

"What?" she finally asked.

Nolan told her what June had told him—minus the revenge not-quite-fantasy part of the tale.

She didn't react at first, and he wondered if she'd actually heard him despite sitting just across the table. She remained frozen, staring at him.

"Bets?" Kenny softly said. "You okay?"

That seemed to break her spell. She blinked her left eye, her right one still swollen mostly shut. "I don't want you two hounded by the press," she said.

"That's not your concern," Nolan told her. "That's ours. And they won't hound us, because they don't know where you are. Even if they did find out, we won't let them talk to you."

"I should probably call my parents and warn them, shouldn't I?"

"Might not be a bad idea."

She held her fork for a moment, motionless, before setting it down next to her plate. "Would it be easier if I just let him skate on these charges?"

"No," both men strongly said, making her left eye widen again.

Nolan softened his tone. "You cannot let him get away with what he did to you. If it goes to trial—and it might not, because he might plead out eventually—we will all be there by your side, with you. You won't be facing him alone."

"He's going to say all sorts of horrible things about me," she said. "I know he will. He used to love telling me the things he'd tell people about me if I tried to leave him."

"Unless you were grinding up live puppies in a blender," Kenny said, "there's nothing he can say about you that will make us think any less about you."

"What if he outs all of you? What if he mentions peoples' names in open court?"

"Just because he says it doesn't make it true," Nolan said. "This is about him beating you, torturing you, holding you against your will." Nolan had a really bad feeling gelling in the pit of his stomach. That maybe, now that she was free of Jack, she might drop the charges against him just to make him go away.

Meaning he'd be free to do this—or worse—to someone else, smarter now in the knowledge of exactly how far he could push a woman without her rebelling, how to keep her firmly under his control.

It sickened Nolan.

Kenny said it first. "How about if he kills the next woman?" he asked, hitting low. "How would that make you feel?"

She stared at him.

"I know," Kenny continued, "that it'd make me, personally, feel like shit. That in the name of you trying to protect my privacy you didn't testify and let him walk and someone died. I'd rather face a few weeks of media scrutiny that would settle down rather than live with the guilt that someone died because I didn't press you hard enough to testify."

Nolan hated the shocked expression on Betsy's face, the borderline hurt there, but he knew Kenny was right.

They couldn't let her back out.

Eventually, she nodded. "I don't want him doing this to anyone else," she said.

"Exactly," Kenny said. "If you ask any of our friends if they have a choice between risking being outed and that fucker going to jail for what he did to you? I know our friends. To a person, they'd all tell you to testify. I can start calling them right now, if you want me to."

"No. That's okay." She stared down at her plate as a long, shuddering sigh escaped her.

Nolan couldn't help that he wanted to sweep her into his arms, hold her, comfort her.

Finally, "Please keep reminding me," she said. "Please keep telling me that." She looked up, first meeting Kenny's gaze, then Nolan's. "Keep reminding me that this is about more than just me. That I have to be the one to finally make a stand."

"We will," Nolan said. "And you won't be making that stand alone. I promise."

* * * *

Thursday morning, Eliza arrived even earlier than Tilly and June had the previous days. The men were still in their bedroom getting their own shower and Betsy went to let her in.

"I have my marching orders from Tilly," Eliza said with a smile.

Betsy had spent a restless night, what little sleep she got filled with nightmares about Jack and what he'd done to her.

About testifying against him.

Eliza's smile faded as she set her purse on the table. "What's wrong?"

Betsy told her what the men had said the night before, about the media.

Eliza nodded. "Yeah, June called us all last night about it." She rested her hands on Betsy's shoulders. "The only way we'll get upset is if you let this guy scare you out of testifying. We're all behind you. The friends who absolutely cannot afford to be exposed to this, they've already protected themselves. This isn't about them. And the prosecutor won't let his public defender take rabbit trails on a case as basic and clear-cut as this. There's ample evidence of what he did to you. This is about if he hit you, abused you, extorted you to keep you there, and held you against your will. Period."

"But what about the BDSM?"

"So? That was between you two. His attorney won't dare call any of us as witnesses for the defense. Not if he's smart. And stop worrying until there's something to worry about. Let's get you ready to go see Ted."

Today was the first day she was able to shave and shower on her own, even though she asked Eliza to hang out in the bathroom with her, just in case. Some of the pain was easing, the swelling was going down in her right eye, and some of the lighter bruises had faded.

The remaining bruises, however, were ugly, dark greenish brown patches, some still purple. She definitely wasn't back to "normal" yet, whatever that meant. Once the swelling in her eye completely disappeared, that would go a long way to her feeling "normal."

Ted was glad to hear that Jack hadn't talked to Betsy's parents. And as Eliza prompted her to tell him about her fears regarding the media coverage, Ted cocked his head at her.

"Do you remember how terrified you were about contacting your parents?"

Betsy nodded. "Yeah. Of course."

"Did that turn out to be a valid fear?"

"No, but I thought it was."

"Of course you thought it was, but it wasn't valid after all, was it?"

"No."

"Then put that same knowledge toward this instance. You don't know if the media will try to track you down, or any of the worst-case things. Ed is an attorney. He makes his living planning for the worst-case scenario. It's kind of what he does for a living, what people hire him for. For all you know, the press might let this die down and nothing else happens. I guarantee you there are hundreds of domestic abuse cases all over this state every month where the abuser tries to say the victim agreed to whatever outlandish treatment they were getting. You don't usually hear about those on the news unless there's a death, or a child gets injured, do you?"

"No." She took a deep breath in and tried to breathe out the stress and fear.

"I have a recommendation for you for a counsellor," he said, handing a card over to her. "I took the liberty of making you an appointment for next Tuesday morning. She's good, she understands the basics of your situation, and she's willing to work with you, understanding you're unable to pay her at this time."

"Thank you."

"Thank us all by staying the course, leaning on us, and listening to us."

"I will."

* * * *

After Ted's, Eliza made a side excursion to shopping plaza in south Sarasota that housed a martial arts school. The sign outside touted several different classes in a variety of martial arts skills, as well as self-defense classes for women and children.

"Why are we stopping here?" Betsy asked.

"Because next week, and every Thursday night, you're coming with me to class," she said as she parked and unfastened her seatbelt. "We're here to sign you up."

Betsy didn't argue, and she somehow managed not to cry when Eliza produced a credit card and paid for the eight-week class for her. The instructor, an older woman who was retired military, scowled as she studied Betsy's face hidden behind the sunglasses and under the hat.

"Is the guy in jail now?" the instructor asked.

"Oooh, yeah," Eliza said. "Couldn't make bail."

"Yet," Betsy said.

The instructor nodded. "Let me know if he makes bail," she said to Eliza. "I'd like to meet him in person and have a little chat."

"You and about half of Sarasota," Eliza said.

* * * *

The rest of Betsy's afternoon with Eliza was spent at the house, with Betsy continuing her job search. She'd received nothing back yet from any of her inquiries except a few auto-responders noting receipt of her application and resume.

She knew it was too soon to feel disheartened about it, but it was difficult to keep her spirits up.

"Maybe I should apply to stores," she said. "Get something while I'm waiting."

"For starters," Eliza said, "it's too soon. You need to heal up. Even if that's what you end up having to do, no offense, it's going to be hard to talk someone into hiring you when they see that goose egg. That might sound harsh, but it's the truth. They don't know you or your history, or that this is a one-time occurrence that won't happen again. They might worry that you'll be calling in more than working because of an abusive boyfriend or something."

"True."

"And what did Tilly tell you to do?"

Betsy smiled. "Keep applying online."

Eliza pointed at her laptop. "Then get to it, young lady. This is the Tilly Says show until she says it isn't."

* * * *

On Friday, Betsy dressed in one of her few pairs of older jeans and a T-shirt before Ross and Loren drove her out to the industrial complex Kel owned. He and Mark Collins met them there, in the vacant unit where they'd left all the stuff they'd moved from the apartment.

"Okay," Mark said. "All you do is say keep, or toss. Let us handle the rest."

Betsy sank onto one of the two scarred dining room chairs that matched the discount-store table. Piled near the unit's door, there actually didn't look like there was a whole lot. Yes, the apartment had been small, but dwarfed by the cavernous empty bay, it looked like less than she'd even had at her previous apartment, which had been even smaller by comparison.

Trying to think ahead, knowing there were some things she might need to keep, she helped them whittle the pile down to about half its previous bulk. The discarded items went into a large Dumpster, with a few going into boxes for Kel to drop back by the apartment and leave locked inside, with her key. The remaining items Kel was going to move into the unit where his office and spare apartment were because he had a prospective renter wanting to look at that unit tomorrow.

Ed had joined them to let her know he'd been interviewed by a Tampa TV station. He also assured her that even though her name wasn't on the apartment lease, since she'd changed her driver's license to that address and had lived there for several months, she met the legal definition of being a resident. As such, while Jack could try to come after her legally and sue her, it was doubtful he would be able to because she could claim the items were hers. And yes, some of them were. Or, had been, before he'd confiscated them and claimed ownership of them, and her.

Retribution would be especially difficult for Jack now with the restraining order against him. An attorney would have to go through Ed to contact her, and Ed had already promised her that he would thwart any attempts along those lines in the most expensive, costly, and time-consuming ways possible, so that any attorney Jack might be able to afford to hire in the future wouldn't even want to touch the case.

"Realistically," she asked, "what are the chances of him getting out on bail?"

He shrugged. "Doubtful," he said. "But I've seen strange things happen before. The judge already denied one bail reduction request. I can promise you that I will do my damnedest to make sure the prosecutor buries whatever poor PD he draws under a mountain of paperwork. I know the woman assigned to your case. She's got a great track record of negotiating pro-victim plea deals for domestic violence cases. And the few that go to court, she nearly always wins them."

"Jack's not going to want to just roll over."

"Maybe not," Ed said, "but if he doesn't, he'll wish he had by the time this is over."

* * * *

Betsy had been sitting on the couch with Loren and Ross and watching the local evening news when Kenny and Nolan arrived home almost at the same time.

That was when a story caught her attention.

"In Sarasota, John Adams Bourke was arrested early Sunday morning on charges of domestic battery, assault, and false imprisonment."

Her blood chilled, everyone falling silent as the female anchor from the Tampa station continued. An evidence picture of the chain, where it had still been bolted to the wall, flashed on the screen as the voiceover continued.

"Police reports state he'd kept his live-in girlfriend, Elizabeth Lambert, chained against her will like a slave. She was finally able to escape from the apartment late Saturday night after allegedly suffering a brutal beating by Bourke, and called friends for help."

The screen changed again, to video of Barbara Stallings being interviewed. "The victim in this case is in hiding out of fear, and rightfully so," Stallings said. "In addition to past injuries, in the most recent attack she'd suffered a concussion, facial lacerations and injuries, and other wounds consistent with a brutal assault. Our office plans on prosecuting this case to the fullest extent."

The reporter interviewing her noted, "The public defender representing the defendant states this is a case of *Fifty Shades* kind of consensual sexual play."

Stallings looked like she wanted to slug the man interviewing her, but she pursed her lips together before finally answering. "There was nothing consensual at all about the kind of severe facial injuries the victim suffered. She had a concussion, required stitches, one eye swollen shut. There is a huge difference between some rough consensual sex play and being beaten up and chained against your will. And I'm sure there's not a jury in the world who will disagree with the state's case there."

The voiceover continued as the picture changed to another shot of the chain, this time of the locked loop that had been around her ankle, dried blood on the links almost looking like rust. "The suspect has not posted bail yet, and at a bond reduction hearing, a judge denied his request. The victim's attorney, Edward Payne, has already filed for and received a restraining order for his client."

The picture changed again, this time showing Ed. "My client has requested, for her safety as well as her privacy, to please be left alone. Even with her attacker in jail, she fears for her safety. She will not be speaking to the media at this time or giving any statements except through me."

The scene switched once again, to video of the apartment, shot through the kitchen window and showing it empty except for a few stray items lying around. "There were suspicions of something amiss even before this." Then, an interview with the next door neighbors.

"Yeah," the man said. "We heard bad sounds sometimes. Almost called the cops a couple of times. But she never spoke to us. She always looked scared. We weren't home Saturday night. I wish we had been to help her out. We came home and there were police everywhere. I'm not surprised, I hate to say. That guy was never friendly. Few times I saw him and her together, he was ordering her around. But it wasn't our business, you know?"

Back to the anchor. "Requests for comment from the suspect, made through his attorney, have not been answered." The camera angle changed, and she looked at it. "A special delivery for a new Tampa mom, whose little bundle of joy decided not to wait, had traffic tied up on the—"

Nolan grabbed the remote and shut the TV off. "Okay," he quietly said. "That wasn't so bad."

Betsy felt like she wanted to scream, to cry, to vomit, but sat motionless.

How many times in the past had a story like that flashed on the TV news, and she'd barely paid any attention to it? Not even ninety seconds, and poof, onto the next story.

Her phone rang, startling her. It was Ed, but she still passed the phone to Ross, who glanced at it before answering. "Yeah. We just saw it...Yes, she did...Okay, thanks." He hung up and returned the phone to her. "It'll probably run again at eleven. He tried to talk them into not giving your name, but they wouldn't make him any promises since it wasn't a sexual crime."

What little appetite she'd had before quickly fled as she stood. "I guess I won't be watching the eleven o'clock news, then. Excuse me, I need to go lie down."

She softly closed her bedroom door behind her. With the help of her friends the past few days, the bedroom was tidy, as if she'd always lived here. No more hastily stashed piles of items. Everything had a place and was neatly tucked away.

It even felt like home.

That scared her.

She studied the shark's tooth, where it lay in a small crystal dish on her dresser. The dish had been one of the few things she'd managed to hold onto when she moved in with Jack. It had belonged to her grandmother, and Jack had let her keep potpourri in it. When they'd returned to the apartment that night to grab her stuff before taking her to the ER, it'd been something she'd specifically asked for, besides her photo albums.

Before she'd moved in with Jack, it'd sat in her living room, on the shelf next to her TV, and had held several rocks, shells, and other little small trinkets she'd picked up over the years.

Things Jack had forced her to get rid of because, to him, they were junk.

Things that had been her life, and meaningful to her.

The shark's tooth was her first new addition to the dish.

Turning, she went to lie down, feeling weary and sad to her very core.

Chapter Fourteen

When it was obvious Jack wasn't making bail, and no one from the media had tracked Betsy or any of their friends down, the next Wednesday, Tilly signed off from LA on Betsy spending the day alone at the men's house, if that's what she really wanted.

It was.

Betsy had known in the beginning she'd needed her friends' love and support and protection. She now needed some alone time to decompress. She also wanted the day alone to process what she'd talked about with the counsellor the day before.

She had a lot of work to do on herself. Yes, before this, she'd had some relationship patterns that weren't exactly healthy, even though they'd never led to anything so violent before. She'd pushed people away, and when she'd finally let someone in, she'd let the wrong kind of person in without taking a healthy stand.

Asking Tilly and Eliza to play matchmaker for her was tempting, but Betsy knew she needed to do this work herself.

After the men went to work, ensuring she'd securely locked the door behind them, she went to take a shower. She didn't even need the shower chair anymore. After she got out, with a towel wrapped around her damp hair, she wiped steam from the mirror and stared at her reflection. While still swollen a little, and bruised, at least now she could completely open her right eye again and see out of it.

The face staring back at her almost looked recognizable again.

Almost.

Tilly had also told her she could take a break for the day from her job search. To spend it taking care of herself, reading, relaxing, even sleeping, if that was what she wanted.

What Betsy wanted to do was help out a little and start pulling her own weight. The men had spent a chunk of the weekend doing chores inside and out, and she felt badly that they'd gently refused her help doing any of them.

After putting on shorts and a T-shirt, she pulled her still-damp hair back in an elastic band and started working. The house wasn't dirty, and the men were decent housekeepers. But there were always things to do. She dusted the living room, vacuumed and mopped the floors, wiped down all the kitchen counters and cleaned the fridge.

Then she cleaned all three bathrooms, did her laundry and theirs, and by the time Nolan got home from work, she had a roasted chicken and side dishes almost ready for dinner, and had brushed her hair out so she even looked halfway presentable.

Her heart nervously fluttered in her chest when Nolan walked in the door. "Oh, hey, that smells delicious." He gave her a quick peck on the cheek before walking down to his bedroom.

Nervous tension ratcheted up inside her, tight, painfully so. She didn't understand why and was trying to figure it out when Kenny walked in the door.

More painful tension.

"Hey, sweetie." Another innocent peck on the cheek. "Mmm, yum. Let me go change."

"Okay."

As the minutes ticked past, she stifled the urge to scream, completely unsure why she felt that way, which disturbed her most of all.

She jumped when she heard the men's bedroom door open, followed by the sound of them talking as they returned to the kitchen.

Then they stopped in the doorway and she froze.

Nolan looked concerned. "Bets, are you all right?"

“I…I cleaned the house today.”

He glanced around, looking confused. “Oookaaay?”

“And did laundry.”

Kenny’s brow furrowed. “Thank you?”

* * * *

The hackles on the back of Kenny’s neck stood up, as if a huge lightning strike were about to hit in the middle of an afternoon storm.

And he was standing there holding a lightning rod.

In the pocket of his shorts, he had the small shark’s tooth necklace for Betsy that he’d picked up at lunch in Sarasota. He’d seen it in a store on Main Street as he was walking back to work, and he’d bought it for her on a whim. It wasn’t expensive, a cheap tourist souvenir, but considering the shark’s tooth she had in her dish, he thought maybe she’d like it.

She was acting terrified, frightened, her body language screaming fear with neon-bright energy.

“Did you want to check what I did?” she asked.

She didn’t even *sound* right, the low, tight tone to her voice sounding nothing like the woman he’d quickly grown more than a little fond of over the past week and a half she’d been living with them.

“Why?” Nolan asked.

Kenny quickly stepped forward, something instinctive in him welling up, protective. His hand slipped into his pocket to find the necklace. Nothing much, just a tooth and some beads strung on a black cord. His fingers closed around it, but he didn’t pull it out yet.

“Bets,” Kenny softly said, “we appreciate you helping out.” He deliberately kept his tone low, gentle, slow, afraid of spooking her in whatever this mental state was that she’d suddenly dropped into.

Tilly had warned them about PTSD. That Betsy might go through it, and that it might trigger in strange, unexpected, and baffling ways, but that they always had to be patient with her when or if it did.

She edged away from them. "If I did something wrong, I'll do it again."

He shook his head. "We don't have any rules about how chores are done. We appreciate you volunteering to help." He heard Nolan start to speak behind him and he held his other hand up to silence him.

"I…I just wanted to help," she said, her eyes growing bright. Tears pooled there, spilling down her cheeks.

"We know, sweetie," Kenny said, slowly bringing his hand out of his pocket, concealing the necklace. "And we appreciate it."

She looked at him, to Nolan, back to him. He wasn't even sure at this point if she realized what she was doing. She trembled, her color poor, pale. He was actually afraid she might be close to fainting, but he didn't want to swoop in, instinctively sure any sudden moves would terrify her, even though he didn't understand why.

"I swear, I'll do it over if it's not right."

He took a risk and lapsed into what Nolan always teased him was Dom tone. "Bets, look me in the eye, sweetie."

She finally did. It broke his heart that he couldn't just *fix* this shit for her.

"Why are you scared, *right* now?" he asked.

Her mouth opened…closed…Then her gaze darted around.

"Bets," he said. "*Look* at me."

She did.

"I'm sorry we're scaring you. What did we do to scare you, sweetie?" And that was the only word for it. Terrified. He didn't know why, but she was.

"You…you didn't." She frowned, and he wasn't sure if she was frowning at him, or at herself.

He tried a trick Tilly had taught them. "I'm going to ask you something, and you need to answer me without thinking about it first. The first thing that pops into your mind. Okay?"

She nodded.

He took a risk and added a little more Dom tone. "*Why* are you scared of us right now?"

"Please don't punish me," she whispered. "If I did the chores wrong, please don't punish me. I don't know your rules. We haven't talked about your rules yet, and I was trying to do the best I could." She broke down sobbing, her hair hanging, concealing her face as she slumped against the counter.

Rage and sorrow warred inside him. He instinctively shifted to the side to block Nolan when he heard his partner's gasp of horror behind him and sensed him trying to step forward. He knew Nolan wanted to do exactly what Kenny wanted to do, and that was protect her and take away her fear.

Only she could do that, though. Only she could work through this.

He had to reach behind him and swat at Nolan to hold him back. "Sweetie," Kenny said, "what did Jack do to you about chores?"

He couldn't see her face through her curtain of hair. "If…I tried so hard. In the beginning, he told me how good I was. I tried harder. Then…it was like every day, even if I did stuff exactly the way he told me, he'd find something wrong. Or change it. Until I never did anything right, no matter how many times I tried to do it, it was always wrong, even if it was right before."

He had to force his breathing to stay slow, steady. "And he'd punish you for it?"

She nodded.

He took another deep breath. "Sweetie, here is our rule about chores, and it's the *only* rule we have about chores—we will *never* punish you about chores. *Ever*. Understand?"

She nodded, but tears still spilled down her cheeks and onto the counter, her body wracked with silent sobs.

He edged forward, slowly, not wanting to spook her. "Not even if you do them badly, not even if you don't do any at all. You have our word, absolutely no punishments about chores. Understand?"

She nodded again.

"Is that why you got so scared when you asked if we wanted to see what you'd done?"

More nodding.

"*Tell* us."

"As…as soon as he got home from work every day…usually…that's what he did first thing. Find out what to punish me for. The…the first…in the beginning, he always made it seem like he felt badly about it. Like he didn't want to punish me…but later it was for fun. I could tell. Fun for him. *Why* did I let him do this to me?"

"Look at me, sweetie."

She finally did.

He opened his hand and held it, palm-up, showing her the necklace. "Do you trust us?"

She looked from it to him and back again, nodding.

* * * *

Holy…fuck. Nolan was desperate to shove Kenny out of the way, to get to Betsy and hold her, but then came the revelations and he realized exactly why his partner had stood firm and not let him pass.

He felt ill, physically sick. And angry.

And protective.

No, June wouldn't get a chance at the fucker if Jack got out of jail.

He'd make sure he took care of Jack himself.

"I found this for you today," Kenny told her in that warm, soothing, but at the same time firm and commanding tone.

Fuck, it even made his cock stir despite the circumstances.

"If you'd like," Kenny continued, "you can wear it as a symbol. A symbol of our promise to protect you and to never punish you. Something you can touch and hold onto when you're afraid, when the fear hits you. Would you like that?"

She stared at it, then at Kenny, then past Kenny to him.

Finally, she nodded.

Kenny held his other hand out to her. "If you trust us, come to us."

Nolan watched as she sucked in a deep, ragged breath before she stepped forward, still crying. Then she reached out and took his hand.

"Good girl," Kenny whispered.

She looked up into his eyes, startled, but now her tears renewed as she folded against him.

He held her, turning so Nolan could step in, too, engulfing her between them in their embrace.

"Such a good girl," Kenny soothed. "You're our *very* good girl. We're so proud of you for trusting us."

Nolan wasn't sure if this was exactly the right way to handle this, the healthy way to go with her fragile emotional state, but if it helped her, he wouldn't argue with it.

She mumbled something against Kenny's chest.

"What was that, sweetie?"

"Is that my collar?" she asked.

Now the men's gazes met.

Nolan honestly didn't know what to say. Kenny had gotten them this far, so he'd let him answer it.

"What do you want it to be?" Kenny asked her.

"I want to feel safe again," she whispered.

"What would make you feel safe?"

Nolan wasn't sure if she'd answer at first.

Then, "I want to be under your protection. Both of you," she said.

Kenny gently turned her to face Nolan and unhooked the clasp on the necklace. Nolan reached up and held her hair back while Kenny fastened the necklace around her neck.

"Then you wear this for us," Kenny said. "When you don't feel safe, you touch it, you hold it. You think about us protecting you. You think about how you trust us, and how you trust Tilly and June and Eliza, and our other friends, and how they'll protect you, too."

Nolan didn't miss that Kenny didn't call it a collar.

She nodded, looking down at it, touching the shark's tooth with her finger.

"We can't make you a lot of promises right now," Kenny said. "But these two promises, we can make and we will keep. We *won't* punish you, and we *will* protect you."

She looked up and met Nolan's gaze.

He remembered exactly how he'd felt the first time he'd looked into Kenny's eyes and knew he loved the man. The visceral shot of adrenaline, the warmth spreading through him, the soul-deep certainty.

Fuck.

Falling in love with her was dangerous. She had a long road ahead of her, and she might not even want them like that when she got to the end of it.

Unfortunately, he knew.

He also knew he'd keep those two promises, too.

"Here's our only other rule right now," Kenny continued. "Never lie to us. We'll never lie to you, and you never lie to us. Okay? No punishments, and no lying."

"Yes, Sir," she answered, still staring into Nolan's eyes, and he wasn't sure if she even realized what she'd said, what she'd added to the end of her response.

She leaned in and hugged him. Nolan looked into Kenny's brown gaze and saw the mix of love and murder boiling there, too.

They were screwed. So, *so* fucking screwed. She didn't even know it.

She was living with two men who absolutely would, right or wrong, kill or die for her, who were falling headlong in love for her…

And who couldn't dare admit it to her unless she made it to a healthier point in her healing and told them first.

* * * *

After dinner, they let her help them do the dishes. Nolan noticed how after she'd recovered from the episode, she seemed lighter, happier.

And she frequently reached up and touched the necklace.

After dinner, they settled in on the couch to watch TV, Betsy snuggled between them, chatting, and talking, and then…

Then she went quiet. When Nolan looked, he realized she'd fallen asleep.

His gaze met Kenny's.

Wow, Nolan silently mouthed.

Kenny sadly nodded.

He'd meant all of it, from her breakdown to how she'd literally passed out sitting there. Exhaustion, most likely.

Neither man had the heart to move and disturb her, but finally, around eleven, Nolan gently spoke. "Bets, sweetie, it's bed time."

She didn't stir at first. He didn't want to startle her by moving, but he and Kenny couldn't spend the night on the couch with her, either. They had to work in the morning.

Kenny grabbed the remote and turned the TV off. "Sweetie, it's time to go to bed," he said.

She finally stirred, looking out of it.

"Bed time," Nolan said.

She nodded, but didn't say anything.

He wasn't even sure if she was really awake.

Moving carefully, the men extricated themselves and stood, both holding a hand out to her.

She stared at them for a minute as if disoriented. For a moment, Nolan wondered if her concussion was having a sudden delayed effect on her.

"Did you both mean it?" she asked.

"Mean what?" Kenny asked.

"That the only rule is no lying?"

The men nodded.

"And no punishments?"

"No punishments," Nolan said. "Maybe one day in the future if you ask nicely there might be funishment *play*, but never, *ever* any real punishments. Not from us. We don't get off on that. If it's not consensual, it completely kills the chubby," he added, trying to lighten the mood.

That earned him a sleepy smile. She took their hands and let them help her up, then they escorted her to her bedroom door, but didn't go any farther.

"Try to get some sleep tonight," Nolan said.

"Thanks. You, too." She reached up to the necklace. "Thank you for this. Both of you. It means a lot to me."

They waited until she'd closed the door behind her before going to their own room. Inside, Nolan fell back onto their bed and stared at the ceiling.

"Holy. Fucking. Crap."

Kenny collapsed next to him. "You can say that again. Who'd have thought a damn five-dollar necklace would bring her out of that?"

"You know we basically collared her tonight, right?"

"I didn't call it a collar."

"I know that and you know that, but I think for all intents and purposes, we just collared her. At least we did in her mind."

Kenny rolled on top of him. "Would that be the worst thing in the world?"

Nolan couldn't stop what he said next. "It is if she leaves us in the future even though we're both in love with her already."

Kenny stared down into his eyes, looking ready to refute that statement when he winced and sat up, straddling him. "Fuck," he whispered. "I *am* in love with her. When the fuck did *that* happen?"

Nolan propped himself up on his elbows. "I don't know, but it did. Now we're screwed."

"Shit." Kenny slumped back on his heels. "Tilly's gonna fucking kill us."

"No, Tilly's not going to kill us," Nolan said. "We might feel like killing ourselves if we fuck this up and either hurt Betsy or drive her away before she's stable enough to even think about something like that with us, though. We have to be even more careful with her. Walk that line of friends and protectors without trying to nudge her into a relationship yet. Not now, anyways."

Chapter Fifteen

Betsy had almost been afraid at first to admit what happened to Tilly when they Skyped the next morning.

Tilly looked tired, even though it was eight o'clock LA time.

Tilly squinted at the screen. "Lean in. Let me see it."

Betsy leaned in closer to the webcam on her laptop so Tilly could get a better look at the necklace.

"But they didn't say they were collaring you?"

She shook her head.

Tilly smiled. "Then it's all good. I'll talk to them and suss things out, but I suspect it was a coincidence, like they said. A fortunate one for you." Her smile faded. "Make sure you write down what happened, though. Talk to the counsellor about it."

"I will."

"Part of me's halfway tempted to order Landry and Cris to go pay that asshole's bail just so Eliza and June can take a whack at him. Along with everyone else." She smiled. "I'd have an alibi. I'm here."

"How do I know if I'm making a mistake?"

"A mistake in what, trusting the guys?"

She nodded.

"If you're making a mistake trusting them, then there are a bunch of us making it right along with you," Tilly said. "It's not like only one of us thinks they're okay. I've known several of their past play partners. They're always on good terms with the guys, never anything bad to say, no rumblings about them, no whispers, no one dropping out of the local scene because of them, or avoiding them. They're the real deal."

Tilly leveled a finger at her in the camera. "But," she emphasized, "remember. If you end up wanting to play with them, don't just go falling in love with them because they've rescued you and you're bonded to them. Try to keep some perspective. There is no rush."

She gave Tilly a salute. "Yes, Ma'am."

Tilly had been taking a sip of coffee and nearly laughed it all over her computer. "Smart-assed subbie girl. Listen to me, I will be the first one to tell you if you're making a mistake. You can always text me if you need to. Call me. Anything. I'll be your voice of reason until you trust yourself again."

"How long?"

"For as long as you need me."

"No, I meant, how long until I trust myself again?" She caught herself fingering the necklace. Yes, she knew it wasn't expensive. And that morning at breakfast, when she asked Kenny about it, where he'd gotten it, he'd told her it'd been an impulse buy the afternoon before.

Coincidence.

A happy one, but still.

"You know," Tilly finally said, "if I had that answer for you, I could make myself rich as a counsellor. I don't have an answer for you. At some point you have to learn to trust yourself again, because in the end, no matter how much our loved ones love us, we are the only ones we can absolutely be certain we can trust."

* * * *

Betsy was ready to go when Eliza came to pick her up at four thirty. As instructed, she wore yoga pants and a T-shirt. The instructor was going to work one-on-one with Betsy for a couple of hours before class, teach her some moves, help her with the basics.

Betsy had never taken a self-defense class before, even though she'd always meant to.

Before.

Then after she was with Jack, there was never any extra money for anything she wanted to do, and the one time she'd mentioned it, when they were having a class at Venture for women, he'd angrily asked if she was questioning his ability to take care of her.

Which had ended up with him punishing her for that.

Her mood swings today, in light of what had happened yesterday, were anger and feeling stupid.

Eliza noticed the necklace. "You might want to take that off before we get started so it doesn't get broken."

"Good point." She'd started to protest, that she couldn't take it off.

That it was her collar.

But it *wasn't* her collar.

Danger.

Yes, she wasn't so blind she couldn't see what everyone was warning her about, not to fall hard for the men because, *reasons*.

Rebound.

Rescuing.

Really damn hawt, but still, no.

Not now.

She removed it and slipped it into her wallet. The only thing in there besides her driver's license and Social Security card.

Not even any money of her own.

She left it in her purse locked in Eliza's trunk and followed her friend inside. By the time they finally left at seven, Betsy was both sore again in body in places she hadn't been sore before, and yet healed mentally in some ways.

The instructor, using Eliza first as her demo partner, had shown Betsy several things. And, of course, Betsy scoffed that she'd be able to do any of them.

Until she did.

By the time class started, Betsy was raring to go, with Eliza as her sparring partner.

She actually didn't feel…powerless anymore.

Jack had been larger and stronger than her. Had she known some of these moves, sure, maybe she could have defended herself. The problem was, she'd willingly let him in and let him mentally and emotionally beat her down long before the impact play crossed the line to physical abuse.

She also knew what she had to do. She did feel safe with the men. She did feel protected with them.

And she did feel attracted to them.

But she would have to first get a place of her own before she could ever commit to them as more than a play partner or friend. She needed to live on her own once more, prove to herself that she could do it.

Now if she could get a job to make that happen.

* * * *

Betsy awoke Friday to an e-mail from Kenny's mom, telling her she had an interview appointment with the company she worked for at one o'clock Monday afternoon. When Betsy read that on her phone, she let out a squeal that must have terrified the poor men, because they came bolting from their room with sopping wet hair and towels wrapped around their hips.

She held up the phone when they ran into the kitchen. "Mom says I have an interview Monday!"

"Hey! That's great!" Kenny gave her a one-armed, slightly damp hug, followed by Nolan. Kenny's mom had stopped by several times for dinner or just to visit with her, to check on her and see how she was doing.

Calling her Mom felt right, even if she did now have her own mom back in her life.

Her own mom couldn't hug her from Virginia, but Michelle could.

The men were just getting ready to leave when Betsy received a notice on her phone of a new e-mail.

She let out another squeal of delight.

The men turned. "Yes?" they said.

"I have an appointment at three today at a real estate place on Longboat Key!"

"Great!" Kenny said. "Make sure you tell us how it goes."

"I will!" She hugged them both, already thinking about what she'd wear. With heavy makeup and her hair loose, it concealed the worst of what damage still remained. She'd decided she would tell most of the truth, because if a prospective employer ran a Google search on her name, it would come up tied to Jack's case.

The Tilly-approved short and sweet version was that she was in the process of leaving her abusive ex to move in with friends when he beat her up. It was honest, it was close enough to the truth to garner sympathy without getting into gory details, and hopefully would let interviewers know she had extricated herself from that situation and it wouldn't prove a distraction to her doing her job.

If they asked about the BDSM accusations on Jack's part, Ed gave her the perfect out there—because it was a pending legal case, her attorney had advised her not to comment on any aspects of it other than what she'd just said.

She called Loren to let her know about it in case that would mess up her schedule. Betsy really wanted the job where Kenny's mom worked, but she would take any job at this point.

Just the fact that she was getting interviews now gave her a renewed sense of hope and purpose.

And when she Skyped with Tilly a little later, Tilly had not only given her a virtual high-five via webcam, but had also helped her pick which outfit to wear.

"If I get the job out there, I'm not sure what to do about transportation," she said. "I don't think the county bus service goes out there."

"Don't sweat it. Lucas and Leigh offered to buy you a car."

Betsy shook her head. "I appreciate that, and please tell them that for me, but that's too much. I need to be able to afford a car and the insurance on my own. You all have already done so much for me and now it's time for me to stand on my feet as much as possible. My parents offered to co-sign a car loan for me, and even that is something I'd rather avoid if I can."

"I can respect that. But if you change your mind, the offer's open."

"Thanks."

"I don't suppose you'd accept borrowing my car, either, would you? It's just sitting there in my driveway."

"Thank you, but I can't. No insurance."

"Ah."

"If I need to, I'll see if I can work out a deal with everyone here for a few weeks, give them gas money and extra money for their time, until I get a couple of paychecks. I'll even take a five-hundred-dollar beater without AC. Do you know how long it's been since I've driven a car?"

Tilly frowned. "How long?"

"Months. Since he made me sell mine. I wasn't allowed to drive."

"Wow."

She fingered her necklace. "Promise me you'll smack me hard in the bad way if you ever see me making stupid decisions like that again, please?"

Tilly held up a hand. "I swear. Except there might be a line in front of me." She smiled.

"That's fine." They fell silent for a moment.

"This is good change," Tilly told her.

"That's freaky."

"I could see the fear in your expression. You're worried, probably for a lot of reasons. The worst that can happen today is you don't get the job." Tilly shrugged. "You're no worse off if that happens. But the best-case scenario is you get the job and it's that next step to you getting Elizabeth Lambert back on course."

* * * *

The guy who interviewed her at the real estate office didn't come right out and ask her about the court case, but Betsy could tell from the questions he did ask and the way that he talked that he was aware of it. Things like her current relationship status, her current living arrangements. Personal questions that had nothing to do with her previous job experience or work skills.

Oddball questions.

It irritated her.

And it set off some interesting warning bells inside her.

By the time she shook hands with him nearly an hour later, Betsy felt glad to be out of the office and back in the safety of Loren's car.

"What's wrong?" Loren immediately asked. "Did you not get it?"

"I don't know. He said he'd let me know next week."

"Then what's wrong?"

"I…" She felt silly. And how much of her feelings were paranoia based on her situation?

Loren arched an eyebrow at her.

Betsy finally went over what happened and her feelings on the matter, feeling even less good about it when she watched Loren's expression darken.

She shifted the car into reverse and backed out. "I don't think this is the job for you," Loren said.

"It's not just me?"

"Trust your gut. If he's asking you questions like that…honey, some of those questions weren't even legal to ask a prospective hire. Like relationship status, things like that. Something isn't right."

Loren swung by to pick Ross up from his office. They were meeting Kenny and Nolan for dinner at a restaurant and Betsy would ride home with them from there. When Loren had Betsy repeat to Ross what had happened, he also looked concerned.

"Yeah, I'm going to go out on a limb here and say if the guy does call you back to offer you the job, tell him thanks, but sorry, you already accepted another position."

Betsy wasn't sure if she should feel relieved or upset by this setback. "Figures it was too good to be true."

Loren, who was now riding in the passenger seat because Ross was driving, turned to where Betsy sat in the backseat and held up a finger at her. "Hey, consider it a test, and you passed. You trusted your gut that there was something wrong, and you brought it to people you trust to talk about it to see if you were overreacting or not. That's a solid win, honey."

* * * *

Monday, Tilly once again helped Betsy pick her outfit via Skype. Loren would again drive her to the interview.

So far, the man from Friday hadn't called back, but she did have an e-mail from yet another agency she'd applied to, wanting to interview her tomorrow at ten in the morning.

Tilly—and Nolan, and Kenny, and pretty much everyone else who heard the story—agreed with Betsy's feelings that something had been off at that interview, and not to take that job, even if offered.

It felt counterintuitive in some ways, because she didn't want to turn down a valid job offer, but if all her friends were saying the same thing, she'd trust them.

Especially since Kenny and Nolan had agreed.

Kenny's mom wasn't doing the actual interview, but she was sitting in on them with the person who was. This interview felt so much different—better and less creepy—than the guy who'd asked unusual questions on Friday. When Betsy finished up with them, she made sure to remember to smile and shake hands with them.

And this time, she gave Loren a thumbs-up as she walked back to the car.

Loren was already cheering for her when Betsy opened the door. "And?"

"I don't know if I got it, but yeah, I get what you all meant now. Even if I don't get this job, the interview felt much better."

"Win."

"Win doesn't pay bills." She fastened her seatbelt.

"You didn't get here overnight," Loren reminded her.

"I also don't want to stay here any longer than I have to."

* * * *

By the time they pulled into the driveway, Betsy had another e-mail, and this one pulled a long *squee* from her.

"Yeah?" Loren asked.

Betsy held up the phone so Loren could read it. It was from the director of human resources at Michelle's work, wanting her to come back on Wednesday for a follow-up secondary interview.

"That's a good sign," Loren said, handing the phone back. "Meanwhile, you still go to the other interview tomorrow."

"Definitely."

Betsy had dinner ready for the guys when they got home. No, they didn't ask her to do it, she wanted to do it. She'd forgotten how much she liked to cook. Jack had a very specific set of meals he wanted, and that was it. She wasn't allowed to improvise or experiment. And usually every meal, even though he'd eaten it, he'd find something about it to punish her for.

She was seeing the common theme and growing more and more disgusted with herself over it.

So much she'd allowed to happen. The old frog in cold water analogy. She'd climbed into the pot and he'd turned the heat up slowly.

Cooking for Kenny and Nolan was different in a good way.

A much better way.

They always praised her efforts and tried to do the dishes. More and more, she was doing chores. Not because she had to, but because she wanted to. As she relaxed and realized they were serious about appreciating her efforts, she found herself enjoying the service, even if it wasn't asked of her.

It made her feel good to do for them when they'd already done so much for her. Because she *wanted* to do for them, not because they asked or expected it of her.

* * * *

Thursday morning, she still hadn't heard anything back yet from the place she'd interviewed on Tuesday. Eliza had just picked her up to head to their self-defense class when Betsy's phone rang.

The funny thing was, it took her a minute to realize what the noise was. She hadn't done a lot of talking on it, mostly texting, and the tone confused her.

Then she realized who it was—Kenny's mom—and answered.

"Hi, Mom."

Michelle laughed. "Just make sure you don't call me that here in the office. Congratulations, honey. They picked you and let me make the call. You start Monday morning."

Her heart hammered in her throat. "Really?"

"Really. Welcome back to the real world."

When Betsy got off the phone with her five minutes later, she realized they were still sitting parked in the driveway, Eliza hanging on her every word.

Betsy burst into tears. "I got it! I got the job!"

Eliza laughed, hugging her. "Oh, honey, I was afraid those were bad tears for a second. Call Tilly, right now! I need to get us to class."

Tilly nearly burst Betsy's eardrum shouting for joy when she gave her the good news. And then they were at class and Betsy didn't have time for anything else except learning how to defend herself.

Michelle had volunteered—refusing any money—to give Betsy rides to and from work for the next two weeks. After that, she'd accept gas money from Betsy, but wanted Betsy to sit down and work out her future budget, including savings, so she could plan for a car.

She was so excited that when Eliza pulled into the men's driveway after class, Betsy realized she hadn't even told them the news yet.

She hugged Eliza and bolted from the car, running inside to tell them.

Apparently, they already knew. Kenny wore a beaming grin as he turned from where he stood at the stove, cooking, and held his arms open for a hug.

Betsy ran to him, throwing herself at him.

"Mom already called me. I figured you were in class. Congratulations."

"Thank you!"

"Don't thank me. Mom said you interviewed better than anyone else, and you already had many of the skills and experience they were looking for compared to the other candidates. You earned it."

"I mean for everything."

Nolan ran into the kitchen. "There's our girl!"

He hugged her, and for a minute it was too easy to envision rising up on her toes and kissing him, kissing Kenny, too.

They all went silent, staring at each other.

"Um, we got you cake," Kenny finally said. "Black forest."

Aaaand the mood was broken.

"Thank you!" She settled for giving them both quick pecks on the cheeks before going to grab a quick shower to rinse off.

Now she'd have to shift into a different gear in her life, back into the workforce while figuring out what to do about Kenny and Nolan.

Because letting them walk out of her life once she was back on her feet was feeling less and less like a good option every day.

* * * *

Nolan listened for the sound of her bedroom door closing. Yes, he was happy for her. Yes, he wanted her to get her life back.

But more and more, he wanted to find a way to let that happen while the two of them stayed a fixture *in* her life.

The two of them looked at each other. "I don't want to lose her," Nolan admitted.

"Neither do I," Kenny said. "But first she has to find herself."

Chapter Sixteen

Except for the classes with Eliza, and going to the counsellor, which now happened on Tuesday evenings, the next four weeks of Betsy's life were mostly filled with learning her new job, making friends with some of the people she now worked with, and doing whatever it was Tilly and the others had lined up for her on the weekends. Twice she'd gone shooting with Gabe, June, and Laura, although she would admit she wasn't comfortable with a handgun the way the other three women were.

She almost felt better with the self-defense techniques she was learning in class with Eliza.

Brooke had taken her to learn archery twice. She'd enjoyed that far more than she had the act of shooting, although being with her friends, even at the gun range, was still something she enjoyed.

Jack was still stuck in jail and slowly winding his way through the judicial system. The state attorney's office hadn't offered him a plea deal yet, wanting him to sit a little longer before they did so he'd have a good taste of what life might be like for him if he didn't get it over with and accept a shorter sentence in exchange for a guilty plea.

And then there was Kenny and Nolan.

A couple of times, they'd gone out to Venture, asking her if she wanted to go.

Before, she'd said no.

She didn't know why, but wanted to puzzle it out first.

That was when it finally hit her.

The men had been nothing but sweet, kind, protective, caring.

And she wanted more.

A lot more.

She'd even been pulling back a little over the past week, afraid of throwing herself at them. While Tilly had been hinting to her that getting involved with the men, now that she was getting her life back together, wasn't a bad thing, Betsy knew the truth.

She wanted them. She needed to be honest with them and tell them that.

And she needed to move out.

She couldn't have it both ways. Not yet. Not now. She could stay there with them platonically forever and never make any progress. Or she could finally reclaim her life…

Including her power to choose who she wanted to be with.

But she wouldn't mire herself in a live-in relationship again yet. Not until she'd been on her own first. And she'd already called Kel and talked to him about what it would take to rent the apartment. She could afford it.

With Jack safely in jail, her safety wasn't an issue anymore.

That Saturday, her friends hadn't planned her schedule for her. The men were eating breakfast when she got up and walked out to join them.

"Are you going to Venture tonight?" she asked.

They shared a glance, but nodded. "Yeah," Nolan said. "Want to come with us?"

She took a deep breath. "Yes. But I want to play."

* * * *

Kenny felt a cold ball of fear rolling around in his gut. "Play with who?" he asked.

She frowned as if she didn't understand his question at first. "You guys," she finally said. "I mean…" Her face turned pink with embarrassment. "I'm sorry," she softly said. "I thought maybe—"

"Yes," he quickly said, feeling like an idiot. "Sorry. For a minute there, I thought you meant you wanted to play with someone else."

From the sound of the relieved breath Nolan exhaled, he felt a little better that he hadn't been alone in his initial confusion.

"No way in hell would I play with anyone but you two," she said. "I'm going car shopping next week after work with Mom. So that's getting done." She rested her hands on the table. "And I've talked to Kel about renting the apartment from him."

The cold ball of fear returned. "Why?"

She met his gaze. "One of our rules is not lying to each other, right?"

"Yeah."

"I care for you both. A lot. And not just as friends. More. But I know that I need to stand on my own two feet again. I'm at the point now where I want to reclaim all of my life. My ability to choose. If you both want to, I want to be play partners with you. And…more."

"More?" He and Nolan asked in unison.

"More." She looked to Nolan, then back to him. "If you guys want to."

He reached across the table and clasped her hand. "You don't have to move out to have us as play partners, or more than play partners."

"I know I don't have to. But I *need* to. I know it might sound illogical. And if I tell Tilly my plan and she tells me I'm wrong, then yeah, I'll rethink it. Two months ago, I thought I was stuck in hell with no hope of escaping. I feel like that was all some horrible nightmare that if I close my eyes long enough, it'll turn out that's all it was. And that's good and it's bad."

Nolan had slipped his fingers around her other hand as she talked, but he didn't interrupt her either.

"It's good, because it means I'm not stuck there anymore. It's bad, because it would be too easy to forget how bad it was, or what got me there in the first place. I can't let that happen. I also don't want to get stuck in a snug little rut here, not taking chances, but not able to really take the next step."

He knew he'd always fall prisoner to her blue eyes, different, lighter in shade than Nolan's and just as gorgeous.

"I would like to get myself to the point where I can one day look you both in the eyes and say I feel ready to be a slave again. Right now, I can't honestly tell you guys that. Bottoming, yes. Hell, I miss a good play session with someone I trust. But if I haven't been reading you guys wrong, and you're both attracted to me, too, then the only way I can make sure I'm going to be giving you the best me I can, the healthiest me I can, is to be on my own again for a while. And while I do that, the three of us can figure out where to go from there. Together."

She squeezed their hands.

"What if you want to date someone else?" Kenny asked, almost afraid to hear the answer.

"That's just the point—I don't *want* to date anyone else. I want to date you two. I trust you guys. So if we're ever going to see what might be possible, that can't happen unless I'm moving on and moving forward."

* * * *

She hoped she wasn't making a mess of things. In her brain, it had sounded logical.

From the unhappy looks on their faces, though, she could tell they weren't pleased.

"So you want us to get closer…by moving out?" Nolan asked.

Okay, not so much. "Look at it this way," she tried again. "Not permanently. I might rent Kel's for a few months and then decide no, I don't want to be away from you guys. But I can't figure that out unless I see. I need this time. I love you both, and…"

She realized what she'd said when the men's heads snapped up, their eyes on her.

"Love-love?" Kenny asked.

"Honesty, right?"

"Yeah," Nolan said, sounding hoarse. "Honesty."

"I need to move out because I'm in love with you both and I need to make sure I'm in love with you because that's how I really feel, or because of the situation. If I move out and still feel the same about you two—or stronger—then I'll know it's real and we can talk about what's next."

Kenny got up and rounded the table. She turned, Nolan next to her, Kenny now kneeling in front of her. "If you're going to do this, then I want a change," Kenny said.

"What?"

He pointed to her necklace. "That now becomes a collar of protection. Our collar on you. And we'll honor it and our commitment to you as long as you do, too."

"And we won't force you to wear it," Nolan said. "And, obviously, it's symbolic, not like if you're taking it off for class or whatever. And if you ask us to end this, we part as friends and do so amicably. Because it would break my heart to lose you as my friend."

She hugged him. "Me, too." She hugged Kenny. "Yes, I accept it as a collar from you both, a collar of protection."

His gaze looked intense, hungry. "Hard limits?"

"Yeah," she said. "We need to talk about those."

"Kissing?"

"What?"

"Kissing. Is that a hard limit, or can we kiss you?"

They'd kissed her and she'd kissed them plenty of times, but as she processed the desire in his expression, she realized he meant more than just the chaste cheek-pecks, or quick brushes in passing of lips over lips.

"Kissing's allowed."

Kenny reached out, grabbed her, and laid a soul-searing kiss on her that nearly made her come right there. Long, volcanic, a kiss better than any she'd ever had in her entire life.

When he released her she'd barely had time to draw in a breath when Nolan grabbed her. His kiss was different than Kenny's and equally as good. If they could kiss this damn good, she suspected the future held even better things for her.

When Nolan finally released her, she felt shaky in a good way.

Kenny wore a playful smirk. "We won't ever order you to stay with us," he said. "But in the interest of honesty, we're not above playing a little dirty to make sure you understand exactly how we feel about you and how much we want you to be part of our lives."

* * * *

The rest of the morning was spent with Betsy in a sexual haze and pleased to see the men's shorts were tented, too, as they discussed in great details hard and soft limits.

For play and sex.

Now having health insurance again, she'd gotten herself to the doctor and tested and back on birth control pills. She'd need another test again in a few months just to make sure, but it was one more relief.

And for now, they'd use condoms.

For play.

And for sex.

Of which if they kept talking about it as in-depth as they were, she was likely to beg them to skip the play and go straight to the sex right now.

But she knew that couldn't happen yet, either. They needed to have these conversations before anything could happen, play or sex.

She agreed that, for the purpose of play and sex, she would be their submissive. Outside of the bedroom or dungeon—or outside of play or sex in general—the rest of her life was absolutely and completely hers to rule and command, as long as it didn't involve her getting involved with anyone but the men. If she found herself in that position, it would put a full stop to everything so they could sit down and discuss it.

She didn't think that would be a problem. For starters, these were the only men she wanted. Her heart already belonged to them.

Getting herself over her fear, her worry about making bad choices? That had nothing to do with what she felt for them and everything to do with knowing to have a successful relationship with them she had to do this self-work.

Tilly called and they took a break as Betsy closed herself in her bedroom to talk to her friend on the phone.

"So what's up for today?" Tilly asked.

Betsy hoped Tilly didn't blow up. "A couple of things." She told her about talking to Kel about the apartment.

Then she revealed what she and the men had been discussing that morning.

Betsy had to look to make sure the call was still connected. "Tilly?"

Her friend's sigh made it all the way from LA. "I'm really proud of you," she said. "No, I can't find fault with your logic."

"Am I doing the right thing?"

"You love them, right?"

"Yeah."

"And you'll be pursuing a relationship with them?"

"Yeah. But I want to make sure I don't end up on the same vicious carousel I was on before when I dated vanilla guys. And I damn sure don't want to end up with another Jack."

"They aren't Jack," Tilly said.

"You know what I mean."

"Then I guess you'd better make sure you do what you need to do. But I'll give you the same warning I gave them—don't fuck up or fuck them over. Don't spend so much time trying to make up your mind that you lose them anyway. Life's too short to play games or waste time."

"I won't do that. I promise. I've wasted enough time in my life. That's why I want to do this, so I can move forward. Hopefully, *with* them."

Chapter Seventeen

By the time they were ready to head for the club that night, they'd ironed out all the hard and soft limits. Yes to sex, across the board. For play, they would start slow and build up. She worried if they restrained her with anything other than their hands that she might panic, memories of what Jack had done to her fresh in her mind. She wanted to be able to build new memories, new trust, and not trigger in a bad way.

At the club when they played, only her men could touch her, and they wouldn't play with anyone but her. They would buy her a play collar to wear at the club, or when they were together privately.

For now, they'd avoid heavy impact play, and no canes. Light impact play, bare-handed spanking, flogging, riding crops, orgasm play.

Yes to all of that.

But the things Jack had done to her, the activities he'd taken and turned into punishments, those she wanted to avoid for now. On her future list of things to reclaim lay those favorite activities, like cane strokes during orgasm play, but not now.

Not until she knew for sure she could handle it.

Or that the men could handle it with her in case she triggered badly.

Tilly must have passed the word around to their friends that they were going tonight, because Loren, Eliza, Gabe, Laura, Brooke, Abbey, and June were all there when Betsy and her men arrived. Not even all their men had come with them. Rob, Bill, Rusty, and Scrye were missing.

Betsy asked her men for a moment alone with her friends and turned to the women once Nolan and Kenny moved out of earshot. "Oookaaay. What's up? This doesn't look at *alll* suspicious."

June smirked. "The first rule about the dungeon is—"

"Shh," Loren said. "We're here for you. And them, too. Because, to be honest? For a couple of guys getting ready to play for the first time with a girl they're head-over crazy about? They look a little depressed."

Apparently Tilly hadn't had time to spread that part of the tale. Betsy filled her friends in, feeling relieved when they all slowly nodded.

"Okay," June said. "Now I get why they look sad. But I get it. Yeah, if you feel you need to do it, you should. Just don't leave them dangling too long out there."

"I won't."

"We're still staying," Eliza said. "Until you guys are done, at least."

"You know they won't violate my safeword," Betsy told her.

"Oh, I know. It's the principle of the matter. Besides, some of us would like to see you play again, because we want to get the memory of how horrible you looked those first several days out of our heads."

"And I'm just a perv," June joked, hugging her. "I want to watch."

* * * *

Betsy returned to her men. "Okay. Now that we have our own cheering section, I guess we can get started."

"June's not going to hold up numbers to score us or something, is she?" Nolan teased. "Because, I swear, she'd be like the Russian judge just to be a pest, I know she would."

"Nope. They just want to see us happy."

The men stepped in close, Nolan in front of her, Kenny behind. She felt hard bulges in both their jeans, but they'd have to wait until they got back home.

"Ready to play?" Nolan asked.

She nodded. "Yes, Sir."

"Get undressed."

With Kenny's help, she pulled off her dress and kicked off her shoes. Then her panties, and she was standing there, naked. The men had put a towel down on the bench for her and helped her onto it.

She didn't want a gag or a blindfold tonight. She needed to feel as safe as possible, focusing on what they were doing to her, not what she couldn't do.

Closing her eyes, she breathed out stress and worry and fear as the men's strong hands stroked her flesh, slowly exploring, feeling, caressing. Yes, it was a little odd that their first truly physically intimate time would be at a dungeon and not alone, but it was better this way. When they returned home, she'd be ready to play in other ways, having had her fears well-allayed already.

Because if this didn't go well, there wouldn't be sexy time later, and the men knew it.

Nolan squeezed her ass cheeks, easing up just before it got painful. Then he lightly smacked her on both ass cheeks…

And it was on.

They almost didn't go hard enough, but she didn't tell them that. They used floggers on her, their hands, a leather strap—nothing she hadn't okayed, and not even some of the more strict implements she had okayed.

Then one of them was slapping her ass—she wasn't sure who and didn't want to open her eyes to look—and she heard the sound of a vibrator clicking to life with a loud hum.

A hand slipped between her legs, exploring, and withdrew. She arched her back as the vibrator then made contact with her clit.

Her fingers curled around the ends of the bench. She didn't bother trying to hold back her cries. She hadn't heard anyone else playing yet and knew she likely wasn't bothering someone's headspace. The hands stopped slapping her ass, leaving only the vibrator and her orgasm.

Kenny leaned in. "That's our good girl," he murmured in her ear. "Just think how good it might feel at home, with one cock in your mouth and another in your pussy at the same time."

That thought only made her come harder. Yes, the fantasy of having the two of them at the same time was now looking like a pretty certain reality.

Oh, sweet mother dick, she couldn't wait.

She didn't know how long she lay squirming there on the bench with Kenny's hands roaming her flesh while Nolan kept the vibrator perfectly positioned. Just as she thought she might have to safeword, the vibrator shut off and the men draped a towel over her.

Gasping for breath, she laid there and tried to process it.

"Good?" Nolan asked.

She nodded, blindly groping for their hands, finding them, squeezing them.

"Great," she whispered.

* * * *

They didn't stay long after that. Once she was up and coherent again, she wanted to get home with them and get busy.

They didn't disappoint.

In their bedroom, they slowly stripped her again, this time worshipping her body with their mouths as they did. Her nipples, her clit, all over, lips and tongues, in delicious, orgasmic stereo. When they finally got naked, she was pleased to see both men were around eight inches, nicely hung, thank you very much. She'd suspected as much from accidental glimpses here and there, not to mention the way they'd felt earlier through their jeans.

Nolan laid back on the bed and crooked a finger at her. She crawled up him, kissing him, loving the feel of his body under her, his length rubbing against her clit.

She felt Kenny's hands between her legs and realized he was rolling a condom on Nolan. Then he held Nolan's shaft, swiping it back and forth through her juices before she slowly impaled herself on it. She didn't know if her moan or Nolan's was louder.

Kenny changed positions, kneeling next to Nolan's face as he leaned forward and kissed her. A moan escaped Kenny, and when she looked, Nolan had Kenny's cock in his mouth.

Her pussy fluttered at the sight as she slowly fucked herself on Nolan's cock. That was, by far, *the* sexiest thing she'd ever seen in her life.

And she'd watched a lot of gay male Internet porn in her single days, pre-Jack.

She reached down and stroked Nolan's cheek with one hand as she reached under Kenny and fondled his sac with her other. Kenny's kiss turned into a tongue-fucking that, added to the way her still-sensitive clit was rubbing against Nolan's body, ended up sending her over the edge.

Something that pleasantly shocked the hell out of her.

Kenny lifted his mouth from hers. "Did you just come?" he playfully asked.

"Mmmhmm, she did," Nolan mumbled.

"I was asking her, not you."

Nolan laughed.

Not only were these two guys hot and hunky, they were fun.

Kenny had brought the vibrator to bed with them. "Guess you don't want this, huh?" he teased her.

"Please, Sir?" she asked.

"Well, since you asked nicely." He switched it on and pressed it to her clit.

Another explosion fired off inside her, drawing an answering moan from Nolan in the process.

"Ooh, that was fun," Kenny said. "Now hurry up and fuck one out of him, baby, so I can fuck that sweet pussy next."

"I thought he was going to suck you off." She kind of wanted to see that.

Actually, she *really* wanted to see that.

"Maybe later. He's just keeping me hard for now. I want to be buried in that pussy and feel you have another one around my cock."

"Do you suck his cock, too?" she asked.

He smiled. "Any chance I get."

She started moving faster, harder, Nolan trying to thrust in time with her until finally he let out a groan around Kenny's cock and his body went rigid for a moment.

"Oh, yeah," Kenny said. "That was a good one, wasn't it, buddy?"

Nolan's head flopped back on the pillow. "Fuck, that was good." Kenny handed him another condom, and he rolled that one onto Kenny's cock for him.

Kenny wanted to be on top this time. He pulled her off Nolan and rolled her onto her back on the bed, sliding his cock deep inside her pussy and making her gasp.

"Yeah, just wait." He grabbed the vibrator, turned it on, and pressed it between their bodies. As he started fucking her, every stroke drove the vibrator against her clit, until one long, rolling orgasm broke free and rocketed through her.

"That's it," Kenny said, pounding her with his cock and for a moment making her forget she was even thinking about moving out.

This. Everything about it was perfect.

Her gaze met his as he came, and he barely managed to keep his eyes open, staring down at her as he slowed and stopped, with a satisfied smile.

She smiled back up at him.

He pulled out and laid down next to her. Sandwiched between the two men, she realized, felt like the most perfect thing in the world.

"How was that for round one?" Nolan asked.

"Round one?"

He kissed her. "Oh, yeah. We'll each be good for at least one more tonight. All we have to do is think about how hot you were on that bench at the dungeon." He brought her hand to his lips, kissing it. "You were gorgeous."

"Beautiful," Kenny echoed.

She smiled, truly feeling beautiful and gorgeous for the first time in a long time. These two men, she knew, were no Jack.

And thank god for that.

Chapter Eighteen

Despite how well things were going over the next couple of weeks, between buying a car and renting Kel's apartment, and both sexy- and playtime with the men, Betsy stuck to her guns about moving. She knew if she could do this thing for herself, carry through with it, at least for a few months, to make sure she wasn't just trading safety for fully healing herself, she and her men would be happier for it in the long run.

And it wasn't like they wouldn't be seeing each other a lot, and spending nights together. But that last little bit of fear in her, she suspected, would disappear if she had a place again that was only hers.

Well, hers and her landlord, but she felt confident Kel wouldn't just boot her out.

She felt the men's sad confusion the morning of moving day, and didn't blame them for it. She could sense how hard they were trying to be supportive of her. She knew they didn't want her to move, but she loved them even more for not trying harder to coax her to stay.

In the kitchen, she pulled Kenny and Nolan's arms around her and kissed them both.

"Guys, remember, this isn't about you. It's about me. I need this time to make sure I'm giving you two the best me I can. I swear, I'm not going anywhere."

"You're moving," Nolan said. "That's going somewhere."

"I'm moving over to Kel's," she said. "Fifteen minutes away."

"You could stay in the spare bedroom here," Kenny said.

"And I'd still be here. You guys can spend the night with me there, whenever you want. But..." She tried to think of how to phrase it. "There's still a little part of me that's chained up in that duplex living room," she said. "And I need to get it back. All of me."

"You have feelings for Jack?" Kenny asked, sounding shocked and hurt.

"No! No, that's *not* what I meant at *all*. I need to let my body and mind settle in and heal. I don't want to wake up in your house five or ten years from now, terrified that I fell for you guys because I wasn't strong enough to be on my own. Does that make sense?"

"No," the men said.

"Do you love me?"

They nodded.

"I love you both, too," she said. Then she reached up and fingered the shark's tooth. "This is my collar from you both. I meant it. That's what I think of this as. But if you both meant what you said that day, if you were serious that you want what's best for me, let me do this. For me. For all of us. You won't lose me. But I have to make sure I've found the real me."

Unlike the last time she'd moved, where it was an all hands on deck emergency, it was just the three of them. With all the other stuff now in a personal storage unit she'd rented, stuff she wouldn't need because Kel's apartment was furnished, all she'd needed to move were her clothes and things from her room.

In a way, it was reminiscent of her moving in with Jack, only instead of feeling bitter that she'd had to leave stuff behind, she felt free that she had things she loved, that had been given to her in love, and with love, and no one could take them away from her anymore.

* * * *

Kenny knew they couldn't stop her, couldn't force her to stay there.

They damn sure couldn't chain her, literally or figuratively. No emotional manipulation to keep her there with them.

This was something she felt she had to do, and they had to let her do it.

Hopefully on the other side, they would be able to prove to her they loved her and wanted what was best for her.

Tilly had told them to let Betsy set the pace, and the course, and that was what they'd do.

He'd be lying, however, if he said he wouldn't miss her being *there*, with them, and he hoped whatever it was Betsy had to do to finally be at peace happened quickly.

When Kenny and Nolan helped her unload the very last of her things, they sat on her bed as she stood in front of them, holding their hands.

"Thank you for this," she said, smiling. "This means a lot to me that you trust me this much to let me do this."

"Promise us you'll stay safe," Nolan said. "Use the security system. Be careful. I don't like you being over here by yourself at night."

"Kel said it was safe. Tilly and Eliza wouldn't have signed off on it if they didn't think it was safe."

"We're going to worry," Kenny said. "Kind of what we do."

"I know. And I love you both for it." She squeezed their hands. "Tomorrow night, dinner, here. Right?" She smiled. "And more."

"Have fun with the girls tonight," Kenny said, pulling her hand to his mouth and kissing the back of it, tasting her.

"Thank you. I will."

Nolan brought her other hand to his mouth, kissing it. "Tomorrow night, we're going to rock your world."

"I hope so." She laughed, and it sounded like such a sweet, beautiful sound. "And you guys can even spend the night, if you want."

"We want," they said together.

* * * *

Once she'd bid the men good-bye, Betsy sat on the couch in the apartment and closed her eyes, trying to think about the lessons June had taught her that first day out on the beach on Manasota Key.

Hell, if Ted had asked her that first day she talked to him where she'd be in a few *weeks* after escaping Jack, she never would have dreamed she'd be here. Emotionally, spiritually, physically.

Romantically.

As much as she wanted to be sharing a house with her men, she knew she needed to do this. Maybe it was a little overkill on her part, but she needed to be out on her own again for a while before deciding to merge households with not just one, but two Doms.

Two handsome, hunky, sexy Doms, yes.

Two Doms she absolutely trusted, yes.

Two Doms who came Tilly-approved, yes.

But this was for her, to prove she wasn't making a mistake.

Under the same roof with them, romantically, for now, she'd always be second-guessing herself. This way, she could be as crazy as she wanted with them and still have her own sanctuary to which she could retreat.

Would she one day move from here back to their house?

Signs point to yes.

Then again, she might save up a little, get a regular apartment somewhere, and live there for a year first.

But the point being she had a *job*. She had a life again. She had a *car*.

She had hope and freedom, and giving all of that up this soon wasn't something she thought was very smart.

Taking to heart what Tilly and Ted had both said, she'd devoured the self-help books on the Kindle. That was another point, while she didn't have people to pay back financially, she needed to make sure she took steps to make them proud.

Not for their sake, but for hers. To pay them back in the only way they would let her pay them back, living proof that their faith in her, their trust in her, hadn't been misplaced. That she wasn't some emotional wreck just bouncing from harbor to harbor once she'd been torn free from her secure moorings by the hurricane that had been Jack Bourke.

Tonight, in *her* apartment, she'd be cooking dinner for Eliza, June, Gabe, Laura, Brooke, and Loren. Tilly would be joining them from California via Skype. Not quite the same thing, but close.

She wanted tonight to be about her being able to personally thank these women. Her tribe, her band of adopted sisters who'd not just given her help, but strength and hope as well.

And first, to do that, she needed to go grocery shopping.

* * * *

Nolan didn't speak much after they got home. The house felt lonely, empty without her there, when before her arrival he'd never noticed the gaping voids of quiet before.

He didn't feel like cooking dinner, and neither did Kenny. They both scrounged for themselves, sitting in front of the TV and eating without talking.

Loneliness.

Yes, they had each other.

But it felt like part of them was now gone, even if they were getting more of her back in the process.

She wasn't *here*.

"What if she decides she doesn't want to come back?" Nolan asked. "What if she decides she likes it better on her own?"

"That's a chance we have to take. She knows how we feel about her. We have to trust her that she's telling us the truth about how she feels about us. We can't force her to stay with us."

He set his plate on the coffee table and laid over, his head in Kenny's lap. "Please tell me this is going to work out all right."

Kenny set his plate on the coffee table, too, and stroked Nolan's hair. "It's going to work out all right."

Nolan laced fingers with him. "Please tell me she's still going to want us when she figures out what it is she needs."

Kenny looked down into his eyes, those sweet, deep mocha eyes of his. "She's still going to want us, because we're still going to want her. This is only temporary. And we'll be spending tomorrow night with her."

"It's not the same. She's not *here*."

* * * *

Kenny knew he had to keep it together for Nolan's sake. Honestly? All he wanted to do was curl up in a ball and cry. Logically, yes, he knew she wasn't "gone."

But like Nolan had said, she wasn't "here," either.

And despite what he'd assured Nolan, no, he had no crystal ball. All he could count on was their promise from her not to lie to them.

And if she was telling them the truth, then this was just a temporary transition she needed to make to be healthy and happy with them later.

She still was "theirs." Their submissive. Kenny kept his hopes high that she would return to them permanently. And if she did, he'd ask her if she'd become their slave, a commitment to them, their commitment to her.

He stroked Nolan's cheek. The man hadn't shaved that day, and a light spray of stubble covered his face. "Love you."

"Love you, too."

Kenny leaned in and kissed him. It reminded him of the early days, when they were still exploring, still learning each other, what they liked, what turned the other's crank. After a few minutes, Nolan rolled over and Kenny helped him open the front of his shorts. Nolan fished Kenny's cock out and started sucking it while Kenny stroked the back of his head.

Closing his eyes, he focused on the feel of Nolan's mouth on his cock, sucking, licking, trying not to compare and contrast him to Betsy's soft skin, smooth cheeks, silky mouth.

"Don't get me all the way off, buddy," Kenny said as he reached down Nolan's body and squeezed his cock through his shorts. "Just get me hard enough to fuck you."

Nolan let out a soft groan as Kenny squeezed his cock again. It grew harder under his fingers. "Yeah, right here," Kenny said. "Gonna fuck you right here. Have you sit on my cock and fuck your sweet ass on it while I stroke your cock."

Another groan from Nolan, this one deeper, more throaty. Yes, Nolan was in the zone.

He tried not to think about how the only thing better would be Betsy sitting on his other side, kissing him right now.

After a couple of minutes, he grabbed Nolan by the back of the hair and forced him off his cock. "Go get the lube and stuff and bring it back here," he said in Dom tone, watching the way Nolan's eyes looked heavy, glazed.

Tonight, his guy needed a mental break. That was fine, he'd give it to him. That was what being in love and being partners was all about, the give and take.

Nolan stumbled up off the couch and headed to the bedroom. Kenny stood, stripped, and then sat down again. He fisted his cock and slowly stroked, trying to keep himself hard.

He couldn't shut his brain off tonight. He couldn't stop worrying about Betsy, couldn't go park outside the apartment and sleep in his car without her knowing, so he could assure himself she was safe.

He couldn't.

She was an adult and needed this.

He'd have to give it to her.

Nolan returned, naked and with everything they'd need. Kenny spread his legs and pointed at the floor in front of him. When Nolan knelt, Kenny grabbed his hair again and leaned in. "Worship my cock first before you put the condom on."

Nolan didn't need to be told twice. He went down on Kenny again, all the way to the root, laving his tongue over it and making him even harder. Then he finally ripped open the pouch and rolled the condom on him, slathering Kenny's cock with lube. He lubed himself, wiped his hands on the towel, then straddled Kenny's lap.

Kenny grabbed Nolan's ass cheeks and held them apart as his lover slowly lowered himself onto Kenny's cock.

"That's it," Kenny told him, watching him do it, his gaze never leaving Nolan's face.

The other man's eyes had dropped closed, lower lip caught under his teeth as he slowly impaled himself. The head of Kenny's cock breached his rim and he started rocking, slowly, gaining a little more ground each time before he finally settled all the way on Kenny's lap.

Kenny smacked Nolan's ass. "So, so fucking good," Kenny said. He reached up and played with Nolan's nipples. When Nolan tried to reciprocate, Kenny stopped him. "Hands behind your back."

Nolan complied.

"That's good." He watched Nolan's cock twitch, pre-cum pearling at the slit. "Slowly fuck my cock," Kenny ordered.

Nolan began a slow, rhythmic rocking, the long, deep strokes he knew Kenny wanted. Kenny wrapped his right fingers around Nolan's cock, sweeping the pre-cum from the head and licking it off his fingers before fisting it again. He rested his other hand on Nolan's hip, slowing him down, guiding his motions, his speed as he began stroking Nolan's cock.

"Let me set the pace," Kenny said. "I want to do this together." He knew his lover's body almost as well as he knew his own. He knew when to speed up, when to take firmer strokes with his hand, when to thrust up a little on the bottom of a stroke with his hips to get a little more of his meat deep inside him.

Nolan's blue gaze had totally glazed over as he stared down into Kenny's eyes. Yes, like this, they were equals because of trust. They could take turns giving and taking when the other needed it. It didn't make either of them any less Domly for it.

It made them human. It made them stronger. Individually, and as a couple.

Hopefully, when Betsy worked through what she had to, it could be the two of them giving her everything she needed from them.

Nolan's ass tightly fisted Kenny's cock, drawing him closer to release as Kenny pumped Nolan's cock with his hand. Finally, Kenny felt his own climax close and started stroking Nolan faster, harder.

About the time Kenny's cock exploded, Nolan let out a long, low groan of his own as his cock spasmed in Kenny's hand. His cum went everywhere, all over Nolan, all over Kenny. Kenny smiled, gently milking a few last drops from him.

"Ahh," Kenny said.

Nolan's eyes had fallen shut. His partner smiled, but it looked sad and worn.

Much the way Kenny's heart currently felt.

"Love you," Kenny said.

Nolan leaned in and kissed him. "Love you, too. Now I guess we need a shower."

"That would be a yes."

Chapter Nineteen

Betsy was wrong. She'd thought the most terrifying life of her night had been the Saturday she'd freed herself and escaped from the apartment.

But facing Jack in open court…

Tilly squeezed her right hand, while Nolan held her left. Behind her, Kenny stood with his hands resting on her shoulders. Ed would have to be the one to stay with her, because both Nolan and Kenny were witnesses to what Jack had done to her.

A bailiff started to lead her away when she sat up with a loud, gasping croak that woke up both men lying in bed with her.

As the nightmare faded, she tried breathing, tried to focus, to use all the tricks and tips June had taught her.

Kenny and Nolan put their arms around her. "More nightmares?" Kenny asked.

She nodded, inhaling the scent of him, of Nolan.

"Less than two weeks, and it'll be over," Nolan said.

"I'll feel better when it's over."

So far, Jack had spent the last several months steadfastly refusing a plea deal. Lately, Kenny and Nolan had spent nearly every night with her at the apartment as her nightmares grew worse.

It'd been three months since she'd moved out of the men's house, but she felt closer to them than ever. She knew she loved them, and she even caught herself thinking and talking about future plans with them as if being together was a certainty.

This close to the trial date, all she wanted to do was get past it and then she could focus on her men and her life.

No denying it, her men were her life. In all the best possible ways. They hadn't once begged or pleaded or ordered her to make up her mind. They focused on current plans, focused on her.

She just…

She needed that last bit of closure.

As she laid back down to try to go to sleep, she knew that even if the trial was delayed, that was still when she would tell her guys she wanted to move back in with them.

This time, for good.

If she couldn't tell they were the right men for her in three months, she never would.

And as far as she was concerned, they were the only ones she wanted.

* * * *

The next Saturday morning, June arrived promptly at five a.m. to pick up Betsy. Last night, the night before, the men had stayed until ten, when she'd finally, gently sent them home. June had made a point of asking her to spend this day with her, and Betsy didn't want to tell her friend no when she suspected there was a deeper plan.

"You realize I wouldn't be doing this for anyone but you, right?" Betsy asked after she locked the front door and got in the passenger side of June's car.

"Not even Tilly?"

"Well, okay, maybe Tilly. And Eliza. And you know what I mean. It's Saturday." She'd brought a travel mug of coffee with her and sipped at it. "Where are we going?"

"You'll see."

"This better be good."

"It will be."

June had told her to dress appropriately yoga-ish, whatever that meant. That they would be outdoors.

As they headed south, Betsy started to get an inkling of where they were heading. When June turned onto Manasota Beach Road, Betsy knew.

"We're going to Blind Pass Beach, aren't we?"

"Sunrise tai chi. Then we're taking a nature walk down at Stump Pass Beach park."

"Why?"

"Because it's there."

"Why this early? We're on Florida's Gulf coast. How about sunset tai chi? There's a great idea."

"No bitching. You're stalling. It's been three months now since you moved out, and you're terrified to make a decision."

"Ah, Tilly sicced you on me."

"Duh. Look, the trial is in a little over a week. Then, you're free."

"If he's convicted. Everyone said he'd cop a plea by now."

"And he still might. What's the latest from Ed?"

"He gets back from vacation late tomorrow. He'd planned it before all this shit hit."

"Your guys deserve an answer."

Yes, they did. They usually spent at least two nights a week together overnight, and saw each other at least four or five nights a week. Sometimes more.

It wasn't much different than living together, except on the nights they didn't stay she sometimes rolled over into a cold, empty, lonely stretch of bed that would have felt much better had there been a Kenny- or Nolan-shaped mass laying there.

Except for the nightmares. Because of them, except for last night, they'd spent most every night with her over the past couple of weeks.

She always slept better with them than without them.

"I'm going to talk to them next week."

"What if the trial gets delayed?"

Betsy shrugged. "No, next week. If I can't tell that those two guys are the loves of my life and nothing like Jack in three months, I'll never get it through my thick skull."

"Hallelujah! Tilly will be so happy." She pulled into the county park's parking lot. They locked their purses in the trunk of the car, grabbed their yoga mats, and in the grey, pre-dawn twilight headed across the road with a few others toward the beach.

* * * *

Kenny had been having a dream that Betsy had finally moved back in and the three of them were celebrating when some godawful, annoying alarm rousted him from what had been turning into a perfectly good wet dream.

"Answer your fuckin' phone," Nolan griped.

Oh, yeah, that was his phone ringer. He finally fumbled around and grabbed it. "Hello?"

"Kenny? Is that you?" He didn't immediately recognize the man's voice.

"Who the hell is this?"

"It's Ed Payne. Where's Betsy? Is she with you?"

Cobwebs blasted out of his brain, between Ed's tone of voice and the mention of Betsy's name. "What's going on? Do you know what time it is?"

"What's going on?" Nolan mumbled. Kenny shoved him to shut him up and switched on the lamp on his side of the bed.

"I know it's fucking goddamned dark thirty here in motherfucking Mexico," Ed said. "But I haven't been near Wi-fucking-Fi to get a motherfucking signal to check my voice mails in a couple of days until now. We just arrived at our fucking hotel here from our trip out to the fucking ruins last week. We're here until tomorrow morning. I'm sweaty, I need a fucking shower, I'm exhausted, and now I'm royally fucking pissed off after getting this news. Now where. The fuck. Is Betsy?"

That the attorney had just used more f-bombs in the past several seconds than Kenny had ever heard him use in the all the years he'd known him scared him shitless. "She's at Kel's apartment."

"And you're *not* there?"

"No, we're home. What's going on?"

"Fuck me, get her on the phone, right now, and get your asses moving over there. He's out on fucking bail."

"*What*?"

Nolan sat up. "What?"

As Ed talked, Kenny stood and rounded the bed, grabbed Nolan's phone from the bedside table, punched Betsy's number in, and shoved the phone at him after he hit connect.

"The state attorney's office didn't call me on my sat phone like I told them to if there was a development," Ed said. "They couldn't stop him from making bail."

"When did this happen? What about the bond reduction being denied? He goes on trial next week!"

"No *shit*, Sherlock. Apparently one of his relatives died and there was some money, and someone was dumb enough to post the original bail amount for him. He's been out since late Wednesday your time."

"Shit!" He looked at Nolan, who held up his phone and shook his head. Kenny circled a finger at him, indicating for him to try again. "Fucking *Wednesday*?"

"Yeah. As soon as you have eyes on her, call me at this number. Write it down, it's my sat phone." Kenny ran out into the kitchen and grabbed the notepad from the counter to write it down. He repeated it back.

"Good. As soon as you are with her. I'll be waiting."

Nolan had followed him down the hall. "What's going on? He made bail?"

"No time. Get dressed." It was almost six thirty. "We have to go over there."

"She won't be there," Nolan said. "June was picking her up early this morning for a girl's day, remember?"

"Call June. If you can't get her, call Scrye, wake his ass up. We still need to get over to the apartment."

Fear had completely blown what little remnants of sleep had remained totally out of his system. He ran back to the bedroom and pulled on clothes as Nolan trailed behind him.

"June's voice mail picks up."

"Leave her a message. Call Betsy's phone back, leave her one, too. Let's get moving."

* * * *

Kenny didn't know if he should feel relieved or even more worried when they arrived at the apartment and found no sign of either woman there. June's car was gone, and Betsy's sat parked in her usual spot. There were no signs of anything being amiss, except the coffee in the pot was still warm even though the machine had been shut off.

They'd gotten Scrye on the phone, who said he'd try them, but he didn't know where they'd went, other than morning tai chi on the beach, and then a planned nature walk.

Fuck, as if there weren't hundreds of miles of Florida Gulf beaches stretching in either direction.

Scrye was going to look through June's calendar and laptop browser history to see if there were any clues. He suggested they call around to some of the other women to see if they knew where the pair had gone.

Unfortunately, three calls later, and they still didn't know. Plus they'd discovered from Loren, call number three, that Tilly was back out in LA.

"Call Tilly," Loren said. "She'll know if anyone will. I don't know anything other than what Scrye told you."

"How can you guys *not* know where they went?" Kenny practically screeched.

Loren sounded more awake now. "Look, I know you're scared, but that's not helping. We're friends. We're not each other's mommies. I couldn't tell you where the place is Eliza takes her for the self-defense classes, either. Or the name of the gun range Laura and Gabe took her. There's something else, call Bill and Gabe. They're law enforcement."

He hated to do it, but while Nolan called Bill and Gabe, he called Tilly.

She answered on the third ring, her voice thick with sleep. "God*dammit*, Cris, I told you, I'm still in fucking LA until Tuesday. If you've called me from New York and woken me up *again*, I'm going to beat you mysel—"

"Tilly, it's Kenny."

There was a pause. Then, it sounded like a totally different woman was speaking to him. A wide-awake and wary woman. "What's wrong? What happened?"

"Where did June take Betsy this morning?"

"What? What the *hell* is going on?"

"Tilly, it's important. *Please*, do you know where June and Betsy went?"

"Some beach thing. Why?"

He nearly burst into tears of frustration as he told her what had happened. When he finished, it sounded like Tilly was up and moving.

And she was now definitely awake. "Motherfucking goddamned dickcheese asshole fucking *fuckwads*!" She took a deep breath and let it out. "Okay, let me think. Hold on." It sounded like she was tapping on a computer keyboard. "Bets sent me some pics once, of a beach.

Said it was the first place June had taken her, and she liked to go there."

"Which one—"

"I'm *working* on it!" More tapping. "I don't remember off-hand, sorry. They've got to be in my e-mail. Hold on."

He looked over at Nolan, who shook his head from where he was talking to someone.

No luck there.

Finally, Tilly said, "Okay, got 'em. Let me look at them."

More waiting.

"There's no ID on them," Tilly said. It's definitely not Siesta Key or Longboat Key, though. I can tell you that. If I had to guess, it's Venice, maybe? No, wait, the public beach there doesn't look like that."

An epiphany struck. "Manasota Key?" Kenny asked. He remembered Betsy mentioning something about it.

"Fuck. Hold on." More tapping. "I can't find an exact match of the pic, but yeah, it could be. Either the north or middle parks. I don't think it's the southern one. My money's on the middle park. I can't remember what it's called."

He would have to remember to give her a hug and kiss of gratitude next time he saw her. "Thank you!"

"Hey! You find her, you call me *before* you fucking call Ed, got it?"

"Deal." He hung up on her and grabbed Nolan. "Talk in the car. Tell Bill I think they're on Manasota Key."

* * * *

"Why do we bring yoga mats if we're not doing yoga?" Betsy asked June as they trudged back to the car.

“In case we want to sit. They don’t blow around like towels do. Do you need your purse?” She opened the trunk and tossed her rolled mat in.

“No.” Betsy added hers to it. “We’re just getting back out again in a few minutes, right?”

“Yep.” It was after seven, and a gorgeous morning. With the windows down and the radio cranked, they drove south, the tangy salt breeze filling the car and lifting Betsy’s spirits. Earlier, she’d felt an odd sensation she couldn’t shake. June had teasingly assured her it was Betsy’s aversion to early mornings.

But now…now she felt alive, awake. She held her hand out the window and surfed the wind with it, flowing up and down, smiling.

“You know,” Betsy said, “I think maybe tonight when the guys come over I’m going to have a talk with them.”

“Yeah?” June asked. “And?”

“Maybe it would be better to face the trial with them than without them. I mean, *living* with them. I know they’re going to be there with me for the actual trial.”

“I think that’s a very smart idea, lady.”

They pulled into the small parking area for Stump Pass Beach State Park at the far southern end of the key. Somewhere to the north, they heard several sirens blaring as deputies or fire trucks or something blasted from the mainland, over the Tom Adams bridge and onto the causeway, heading toward the key. In the still, early morning air, the sound traveled for miles. They could also clearly hear outboard motors of boats in the Intracoastal making their way toward open water.

“Holy shit,” June muttered, listening. “Something’s happened.”

“Are we going to walk or stand here?” Betsy swatted at a noseeum. “We stand still too long, we’ll get carried away.”

“It’ll be better by the water,” June said as she led the way after locking the car and tucking the keys into her pocket.

They were on the trail when Betsy *tsked.* "I should have brought my phone and taken pictures for Tilly."

"You want to go back and get it?"

"No, that's okay. I don't want to walk back. Let's keep going."

They headed south along the trails. There were a few people, but most of them walked along the shoreline, heads down and looking for shells.

"Thank you for this," Betsy told her. "I needed to clear my head."

"Duh." June smiled at her. "You'd sort of gotten yourself stuck in a different kind of rut," she said. "You needed to be shaken out of your routine again."

"I don't know what the hell I'd do without you guys," Betsy said. "I love you."

"Love you, too. We all do. That's why we've been so heavily vested in not just you, but the guys, as well. The three of you are perfect together. You have to be the one to make the call, though."

"Yeah. I got scared again."

"Afraid to take another chance."

"Isn't that stupid?" Betsy paused to take a deep breath. "I was stuck in Hell, then I ended up in Heaven, and then I stuck myself in Purgatory."

"I wouldn't look at it like that. You needed to decompress for a while. The guys were your safety net when you crashed. You needed to recalibrate your wings, or some pilot shit like that. You have. Now you can go fly again."

"Some pilot shit like that?"

"I don't know. I'm a gymnast, not a pilot." They started walking again. "In training, you get these peaks and valleys. Sometimes, you hit plateaus. You might have something nailed and then, suddenly, something stops working, and you couldn't nail that flip or stick that landing to save your life. That's when a good coach will make you stop and do something different. Either try it from the other side of the bar than you're used to, or reversing your routine direction on the mats, something drastically different, even if it's technically wrong to do it that way, to see if that makes any changes to what's not working."

"And if it doesn't?"

"You try something else. But the point is, once you *do* get your mojo back, you go back to doing it the way you're supposed to." June shrugged. "I think the way you're *supposed* to be doing things is living with Nolan and Kenny. If they were two guys I didn't know from Cheech and Chong, obviously my advice would differ greatly. But we all know them and trust them."

"Aaannd they're terrified of Tilly," Betsy joked.

"No, they're just intimidated by Tilly. They're terrified of *me*."

"You?" Betsy laughed. "Why?"

"Because I'm one mean fucking momma bear. I raised two girls and taught kids' gymnastics for too many damn years, dealing with helicopter parents who couldn't butt out."

They cut back from the beach into the trails again, losing sight of most people as they did. The path curved through scrubby land and into some trees.

"I certainly wouldn't want to go up against you," Betsy joked. She didn't honestly see how the tiny, petite woman could possibly be scary.

Betsy first thought maybe it was a large dog that had jumped out onto the trail behind her. The blur of movement caught her eye and she spun around as June let out a scream.

"Fucking cunt," Jack said.

* * * *

While Kenny drove, on the phone with Scrye and getting the description and license plate for June's car, he was relaying information to Nolan, who was still on the phone with Gabe, who was relaying information to and from Bill, who was on the phone with

Charlotte County dispatchers, who were also on the phone to Sarasota County dispatchers. The damn key was split right across the middle at the county line. The northern two parks lay in Sarasota, but a patrolman who'd been on the key swung through each of them and didn't see June's car or a tai chi group.

So Bill now had deputies scouring the much larger Englewood Beach park, and others heading to Stump Pass Beach State Park. Gabe and Bill were in their car and heading there as well to help with the search.

Kenny had another call coming in and had to put Scrye on hold. "Yeah?"

"Did you find her?" Ed asked.

"Not yet. We've got deputies in two counties looking. She's with June. I'll call you back." He switched back to Scrye, who was now laughing.

"What's so funny?" he asked.

"I owe my good girl a reward later," Scrye said. "Wherever they are, she's packing."

"What?"

"Carrying," Scrye said. "She usually doesn't take a weapon to the beach with her. For starters, depending on where you are, that's sometimes illegal, depending on county or state park rules. And she hates getting sand in—"

"She's armed?"

"Yes. That's what I've been saying. Take comfort in the knowledge that my little tiny Tasmanian Devil of a wife has 9mm hollow points on her person, yes."

"Thank god!"

"What?" Nolan asked.

"June has a gun," Kenny said to Nolan, who immediately passed the info on to Gabe and Bill.

"You weren't supposed to tell *them* that," Kenny said. "I was telling *you* that."

"Oh, sorry. I thought they needed to know that."

"She gets in trouble for having it in a park, *you* get to deal with her," Kenny warned.

"Gee, thanks," Nolan muttered. Then, after a moment, he said, "Son of a bitch!"

"What?"

"Bill said several reports are getting called in to Charlotte County 911, of multiple shots fired in Stump Pass Beach State Park."

"I think we just found your wife," Kenny told Scrye. "You'd better get in the car and head this way. And I think you'd better get Ross and Loren on the phone. She might need an attorney."

Chapter Twenty

Betsy didn't have time to think, her reactions welling instinctively from deep within. It was as if time slowed, her focus narrowed, and then all the training she'd had in the classes with Eliza kicked in.

If she'd ever been allowed a little "alone" time with Jack, she thought rage would be the first, primary emotion she felt.

Hatred.

Anger, at the very least.

Instead, it was like cool, calm dispassion kicked in. She spotted the large knife in his hand, which he'd raised as he lunged toward her. Instead of running from him she twisted, her arms coming up to block him and kicking as hard as she could at his knee from the side.

He didn't go all the way down, but he stumbled with an enraged cry.

She heard June screaming her name, but Betsy didn't take her eyes off Jack. Instead, she dipped at the knees and scooped up a handful of coarse beach sand from the trail, so that when he turned toward her again she rose and flung it in his face in one smooth, fluid movement.

He screamed at her, something unintelligible, flailing blindly at her with the knife.

And still she wanted a piece of him.

June shoved her hard, knocking her off the path and away from Jack and breaking the spell.

And that was when six gunshots exploded, deafening, ripping Betsy out of that cool, calm dispassion and dropping her into the here and now.

When Betsy sat up and looked, June stood between her and Jack's still body on the ground. The small woman, nearly two feet shorter than Jack, was breathing heavily. Betsy could see her chest rising and falling, but not hear it over the sound of the gunshots still ringing in her ears.

Guess that's why we wear shooter's muffs at the range.

Then June stepped forward and kicked at one of his hands, knocking the knife free even as she kept the gun trained on him. She grabbed it with her left hand, picked it up by the tip, and tossed it closer to Betsy.

She stepped away from him and toward her, yelling at Betsy.

Betsy couldn't make out all the words, and June wasn't turning to face her. Finally, June slowly backed up, keeping her focus on Jack, and blindly reached out behind her, feeling for Betsy.

Betsy caught her hand and June hauled her up and to her feet with a strength she didn't think the woman could possess.

"Are you okay?" June screamed.

Betsy nodded, trembling as adrenaline flooded into her system, a little late for the party, but, oh well, better late than never.

Jack lay on the ground, his eyes open, staring at her.

Still alive.

Blood bubbled from between his lips and he looked like he was gasping for air.

June kept her left hand painfully clamped around Betsy's right wrist, holding her there in place and slightly behind her, keeping herself and her gun between Jack's dying form and Betsy.

Several men ran up, and that was when Betsy checked out. Her knees gave out and she sat down, hard, dragging June down into a seated position with her as she stared at Jack and cried.

* * * *

Nolan hoped the scary little former gymnast had finally gotten her wish, but that the women were all right. By the time they reached the park entrance, county deputies and state wildlife officers had shut down the parking area. Kenny and Nolan risked parking in front of someone's house and ran down to where yellow police tape had been strung across the entrance.

When they tried begging the officer to let them in, they heard a man yelling their name and waving at them.

Bill.

The officer let them through, and they charged across the unpaved parking area, toward where Bill stood next to an ambulance and was talking to another deputy. He was dressed in shorts and a T-shirt, his badge holder hanging from a chain around his neck and the print of a sidearm visible under his shirt at his waist.

Betsy sat on the back of the ambulance, sobbing against her friend, while a stony-faced June sat next to her, arm around her shoulders. EMTs stood helplessly by and watched.

"June wouldn't let anyone touch her," Bill said to them as they slid to a stop. "Betsy screamed bloody murder anytime anyone tried to touch her, so June took over."

"Is he…"

Bill nodded.

Two uniformed county deputies, and another uniformed state wildlife officer, stood close by and kept their eyes on June. "They're going to need to talk to June and get her detailed statement," Bill said, "but I kind of stepped in to stall things, figuring you'd be here soon."

Kenny and Nolan slowly approached the back of the ambulance. June didn't even acknowledge their presence, staring past them.

"Bets," Kenny said. "Sweetie?"

She looked up at them, then at June. "Can I?" she softly asked.

That was when June finally moved. She kissed Betsy's forehead and whispered something into her ear. Then June removed her arm from around Betsy's shoulders and she slid to the far end of the bumper, but still stayed within arm's reach of her friend.

Kenny and Nolan gathered around Betsy. "Are you okay?" Nolan asked.

"No, she's *not* fucking okay," June said in that same flat, scary voice she'd used that day in the driveway when Nolan had talked with her. "The fucker tried to kill us."

He turned to look at her. She met his gaze, unflinching, unblinking, her jaw tight and every muscle in her face and neck starkly visible.

They heard more shouting by the gate, a familiar voice, and Bill waved someone else through. The vehicles and angle blocked their view of who it was.

Then Scrye came pounding up, panting, his T-shirt and shorts soaked with sweat.

Nolan would testify in court if asked that June's feet didn't even touch the ground as she flung herself off the ambulance bumper at her husband. He caught her as she wrapped her arms and legs around him, buried her face against his chest, and started sobbing as he held her and stroked her back. He walked over, turning to sit on the bumper next to them.

"May I?" he asked.

Nolan suppressed a nervous laugh. "Our bumper is your bumper."

Nolan returned his focus to Betsy and tuned out the soft whispers Scrye spoke to June, her sobs now nearly as loud as Betsy's had been.

It did seem the tiny, terrifying gymnast had a two-hundred-pound-plus weak spot.

Kenny's phone rang, but he ignored it. Then Nolan's rang, and he answered it. It was Ed.

"You fucking find them yet?"

"Yeah. They're okay."

"Jack?"

"Not so much."

"Good. I'm getting a shower and some sleep. I'll call you when I wake up. Ross has Amanda's weekend number. He'll take care of whatever needs to be taken care of until I get back."

"Thanks."

Two crime scene deputies wheeled a gurney with a body bag on it out toward the Medical Examiner's van. Nolan shifted position, in case Betsy looked up, so she couldn't see it. He glanced over and saw Scrye lift one of his hands and press June's face against his far shoulder, keeping it there and keeping her in place as he continued whispering to her.

Nolan knew he heard "good girl" and then tuned out, sure that whatever was being said was way too private for his ears.

Instead, he focused on Betsy.

Their good girl.

Bill waved someone else in, and Ross and Loren ran up, both of them out of breath. That was when Bill stepped in close. "Guys?" Bill said to Scrye, Kenny, and Nolan. "They have to take their statements. Especially June's."

June sniffled and sat up, wiping at her eyes. "Daddy," she whispered, "they had to take my gun."

Scrye laughed and kissed her. "That's okay. I'll buy you a new one, sweetie."

"You gave me that one."

"I know, and you did good. You did just what I always told you to do. Now, I'm going to sit here and make sure I'm not having a heart attack from that jog, while you and Ross are going to talk to the deputies. I'm going to sit right here. Okay?"

She nodded, unpeeling herself from his massive frame. Scrye handed her—literally passing her hand—over to Ross, who led her over to another vehicle with a couple of officers.

Bill stayed there with them as the other officers started questioning Betsy.

Nolan looked at Scrye, who was mopping the sweat from his face with the hem of his now-soaked T-shirt.

"You all right?"

"I don't know. I haven't run track since high school, and even then I was slower than a herd of turtles stampeding through a tub of peanut butter. I don't think we're going to be joining everyone tonight, though. I think we're going to make a stay-home night of it."

"Yeah, I think we are, too."

The men stared at each other for a moment before they both broke into wide grins.

He leaned close to speak into Scrye's ear. "Remind me to tell you the story where your wife literally made me piss myself in my own driveway a couple of months ago."

Scrye chuckled. "Buddy, I've had a few yellow stains myself over the years. And I'm her damn Dom!"

* * * *

After they finished questioning Betsy, Kenny handed her off to Nolan while he stepped away to call Tilly.

She answered before the first ring even finished. "The first words out of your mouth better be 'they're okay.'"

"They're okay."

"Oh, sweet mother dick, thank you."

"You sitting down?"

"Is this going to require liquor?"

"No, but I suspect you'll want to start packing and fly home."

He gave her the short version, what he knew of it from listening to Betsy tell it. When the other officers had finished questioning June, as he was talking to Tilly, he watched Ross lead her back to her husband. She'd once again climbed onto him, not caring what anyone else thought, and clung to him like a koala on a eucalyptus tree.

In fact, the scale looked pretty accurate.

"Holy fucking shit," Tilly whispered. "Seriously? She fucking *killed* him?"

"I just watched his body get wheeled out of here and into an ME's van."

"Fuck. Me." She giggled. "Is it horrible of me to want to ask Landry to buy June a commemorative gold-plated gun?"

"No, but I don't think she's in a celebratory mood right now." He turned. Scrye was once again whispering in his wife's ear. He couldn't see June's face, but from the way her body shuddered, he suspected she was crying again.

He heard fingers on a keyboard. "You're probably right. Ooh, book that flight, yes, please. I'll be home by nine p.m. Florida time. Keep me posted if you aren't home, because I'll stop at your place first."

"Will do."

"Hey." Tilly's tone softened, snarkless. "Give them both a hug and kiss for me. Tell them I love them."

He glanced at June. "I'll pass the word to Scrye for you for June, but I'll take care of Betsy."

"You're a good Dom, Charlie Brown."

* * * *

By noon, the investigators had finally released everyone to go. From witness testimony and the physical evidence, it was clearly a case of self-defense. Whether June would be charged with having a concealed weapon in a state park remained to be seen, although Ross said even if the state attorney's office did press charges they could likely plead it down to a misdemeanor in light of what had happened.

Although when the media found out who the deceased was and his tie to Betsy, it got…crazier.

Ross had sent everyone home, Loren driving June's car back for the couple since it was all Scrye could do to order June to let go of him and sit in the passenger seat of his car. Ross would go home, get a shower and more coffee, get in touch with Ed and Ed's office, the other authorities, and then get in touch with everyone.

Kenny drove while Nolan sat in the backseat of their car with Betsy, holding her. He took the Interstate back, and when he turned toward her apartment, she asked, "Where are we going?" in a rather shrill tone.

"I was going to drive us to your place and stay with you there, sweetie."

"I want to go *home*," she said. "I want to go *home* with *you*."

His first instinct was to say, "Your wish is my command," and spin the wheel around right there in the middle of traffic.

But he didn't want her to make a decision she'd regret. "We hadn't talked about you moving back yet," he said. "I didn't want to assume—"

"Ask June! I told her this morning I was going to ask you guys tonight. Please, *please*, take me home." She started sobbing again. He caught Nolan's gaze in the rearview mirror and thought his partner was going to punch him for not immediately turning the car around.

"Okay, honey. Calm down. We're almost to the apartment. Let's pull in there for just a minute and talk."

He parked next to her car, put it in park, and then turned.

Nolan glared at him, her face pressed against his shoulder.

Kenny gave him a stink-eye and then reached over the seat to stroke her hair. "We promised you we wouldn't force you to do anything, sweetie," he said. "You tell us what you want."

She sniffled as she lifted her head from Nolan's shoulder. "I'm yours. I belong to you both. Please, I don't want to be alone anymore. I feel safe when I'm with you, and I'm done trying to stay alone. I want to be with you guys. Please?"

"You don't need to be our submissive or our slave to be with us," he gently said. "We love you, and we want you in our lives. If you want to wait on other stuff, we're okay with that."

"Yeah," Nolan said, his expression softening when he realized Kenny wasn't going to force her to stay at the apartment. "We just want you, however you want to be with us."

"I want to be your slave," she said. "I trust you guys. I love you guys." She sniffled again. "Do you know what June whispered to me when you got there?"

"No, sweetie," Kenny said. "We couldn't hear her."

"She told me if I let you two go because of fear, she'd never forgive me, because it cost her her favorite gun." She giggled. "She really said that."

Kenny laughed. "I *can* believe that, strangely enough."

"I think she was in shock," Nolan said. "When Scrye got there, it was like she had a nervous breakdown or something."

"I was pretty out of it before you guys got there." Betsy sniffled. "But I'm pretty sure I heard one of the cops say 'tight grouping' or something like that when they were examining Jack, before they took us out to the parking lot. She got between me and Jack. She was willing to die to protect me, if she had to. If she has that kind of faith in you two and doesn't even know you two as well as I do, I'm done trying to do this shit on my own. I'm choosing you because I love you and life's too short for me to live in fear anymore."

"Tell us what you want, sweetie," Kenny softly said. "You need to ask us."

She took a long, hitching breath. "I want to be with you guys, as your slave. I want to belong to both of you. I want you two to get legally married—because fuck you, assholes who kept holding up gay marriage for so long here in this state, and you two have been together for so long—and I want to be your slave."

Kenny started laughing. "You have been talking to Tilly waaay too much," he teased, leaning across the seat to kiss her.

Nolan kissed her. "Would you do us the honor of being our slave, Elizabeth?"

She nodded. "Yes, Sir." She looked at Kenny. "I would love to be your slave. Both of you."

Kenny reached out and touched the shark's tooth necklace still around her neck. "I wonder if Becca can make something out of chainmaille with a shark's tooth?"

"I have a rule I want to put forth," Nolan said, getting their attention.

"What?" Kenny asked.

"It's an addendum to the punishment rule, so she needs to approve it."

She looked a little nervous, but she nodded for him to go on.

"I get that sometimes you're going to go places with your friends," Nolan said. "I get it. And I also get that, sometimes, you won't have your phone on you, or be able to use it. In the future, please, make sure you throw us a text, or leave us a note, if you aren't going to be in contact."

"Or?"

He thought about it for a moment. "You would have to choose the punishment," he said. "No, we will not use that as an excuse to punish you at will," he added. "And you can, of course, say no punishment was needed. But…come on."

"She didn't know Jack was free," Kenny said.

"I know. Today wouldn't be a punishment day," he said. "Because, reasons. However, I would like to reserve the right, in extraordinary circumstances, to bring up punishment."

Kenny hoped that wasn't pushing the envelope too far.

Betsy slowly nodded. "That's fair," she finally said. "I'll agree to that. But what are you thinking are punishments?"

Nolan shrugged. "Your choice."

"Cane strokes?"

He shrugged. "Maybe."

"Paddle?"

Another shrug.

"Well, what?" she asked.

"I was thinking more like you on your knees, not being allowed to come while you suck one of our cocks and the other uses a vibrator on you. And if you come without permission, you get five swats with a paddle, and then it's forced orgasm torture on you until we say stop."

He watched as she slowly licked her lips. "That's fair," she softly said.

She couldn't fool Kenny. Her eyes had already taken on that sweet, spacey glaze he loved seeing her wear.

"Well, can I make a suggestion?" Kenny asked.

She nodded.

"How about we grab whatever you'll need for the next day or so, and take it home with us, and then you can try out that punishment, just to see if you'd be okay with it or not?"

She nodded. "Maybe even without the paddle strokes?"

"Sure. That's fair."

"Yes, Sir."

Kenny smiled. "Such a good girl."

Chapter Twenty-One

They didn't actually play when they got home. They grabbed showers and snuggled on the couch and had to answer phone calls every five minutes, it felt like.

By the time Tilly arrived later that evening, driving a rental car and having come straight from Tampa International, Ross and the investigators had some answers.

Yes, there was a restraining order against Jack about Betsy. But what Ed had forgotten was that, when he'd originally filed it, he'd included the building's property address where the apartment and club were as one of the specifically prohibited locales. Because they were a commercial property, and not technically a residential property, he'd been prepared to say she was storing her stuff there, had there been any questions asked.

Which, technically, had been the truth, in the beginning.

The men's address had been protected, but no one had foreseen Jack making bail that close to the trial date.

He'd apparently gotten the paperwork from his attorney sometime on Friday about his trial, and had simply used it to start looking for her. He must have seen June arrive to pick Betsy up and followed them.

That was all conjecture, since all they had was Jack dead in the park at that point. The car traced to him at the park belonged to a former coworker of his who said Jack showed up with five hundred dollars and asked to rent the car for the week because he didn't have a credit card and needed to get evidence to prove he was innocent.

Tilly left after reassuring herself Betsy was alive and well. She was heading for Scrye and June's next, just to put eyes on her friend. Tomorrow, they would all come to Tilly's for brunch, including Ross and Loren.

Tonight, they would cuddle in bed, kiss every inch of Betsy's flesh, and give thanks for tiny little former gymnasts with anger issues and concealed carry permits.

At least, that had been Kenny's plan.

It soon became apparent that Betsy had other plans. She rolled on top of him, getting him hard with her hand before slipping him inside her pussy.

She was wet.

Nolan crowded in close. "You sure you're up for this, sweetie?" he asked, voicing what Kenny was feeling.

"Absolutely, Sir," she said.

"Okey dokey," Nolan said, leaning in to suck her right nipple into his mouth.

She gasped. "That's not what I want, Sir," she said.

Nolan's head popped up like a meerkat. "Huh?"

"I want you both."

Kenny and Nolan shared a quick glance before Kenny glanced at the bathroom door, and then back to him.

The coded message there being, "Go get a towel and stuff."

Yes, they had already crossed this bridge early on. She enjoyed anal play, but usually they worked her up to it over an hour or so of playing with butt plugs and vibrator play.

Nolan quickly returned and jumped into bed. Kenny felt him kneeling behind her, and she fell still as he got to work lubing her ass.

She rested her head on Kenny's chest. "I want my Sirs to fuck me hard tonight," she said.

Kenny reached up and brushed the hair from her face, holding it out of her eyes, searching her gaze with his. "Are you all right?"

She nodded. "Life is too short," she said. "No more wasting it."

After a few minutes, she was rocking back and forth on Kenny's cock in her pussy and Nolan's fingers in her ass. "Ready for more, baby?" Nolan asked her.

"Yes, Sir."

The sound of a condom pouch being ripped open was followed seconds later by Betsy falling still.

Then Kenny felt it as Nolan worked his cock up her ass. Once they were both deeply buried inside her, she started slowly fucking herself on their cocks, leaving them to fill in.

And normally, like this, she liked a vibrator tossed into the mix to help her get over faster. Not tonight. Tonight, she was apparently determined to ride this one out *au naturel*, so to speak.

He reached up and played with her nipples. That was rewarded by her breath quickening, her pace growing faster as she fucked them harder, deeper, until she was close. He could feel the tension ratcheting inside her body like a rubber band, close to snapping. When it finally did, she threw her head back and let out a cry that sounded somewhere between triumph and pleasure before the men started moving, fucking her, catching up to finish with her, leaving them all breathless and weak and utterly satisfied.

As they all snuggled together, she closed her eyes. "Thank you, Sirs," she whispered. "You both have always taken such good care of me. I love both of you."

Kenny kissed her. "Love you, too, sweetie."

Nolan did the same. "Love you, baby."

The men shared a long, sweet kiss. "Love you, Sir," Nolan teased. "You're faaabulooouuus."

Betsy giggled, and that was probably the best sound Kenny had heard in his entire damn life.

Chapter Twenty-Two

"Everyone ready?" Leah asked?

After getting thumbs-ups from everyone, Leah hurried back outside to where they were holding the wedding. Loren was officiating the vows between Kenny and Nolan.

And Betsy.

And Nolan's parents still weren't exactly sure why their son was legally marrying Kenny, yet the girl who seemed to be their girlfriend was also wearing a wedding dress. Likewise, Betsy's parents were a little confused about why Nolan and Kenny were getting married when they thought, but still weren't sure, that Betsy was marrying Nolan or Kenny.

The rest of the wedding party pretended it was the most natural thing in the world.

Which, of course, to them, it was.

This was as vanilla as it got in their group. They were holding the wedding at Lucas, Leigh, and Nick-2's house. Fitting, because that was where Nolan and Kenny had been the night Betsy really walked into their life to stay.

Only a select group of close friends from the Suncoast Society were invited, and all of them had been at the party that night as well. And the family.

Only Kenny's mom was totally in the know and did her best to help the other sets of parents through it all.

Dennis was on a cruise to Mexico with a buddy of his, a Christmas gift to her husband.

And it happened to coincide with the date of the wedding.

How convenient.

Leigh, bless her heart, was waddling around, trying to make sure everyone was being taken care of. Tilly was busy chasing after her, trying to order her to get off her feet.

They all gathered together. "Any comments before we get started?" Loren called out.

"Does anyone need the duct tape?" Gilo called out, making everyone except the parents laugh, and only because they weren't in on the joke.

"Nope, I think we're good there, Gilo," Loren said, obviously trying not to bust out laughing. She seemed to need a moment to compose her thoughts. "I know you three have your vows and said I could say whatever I wanted," she started. "So, for starters, you two are married," she said, indicating Kenny and Nolan with a smile. "Let's just get that right out of the way, because even though it's the legal part, it's not the important part."

Around Betsy's neck, she wore a gorgeous, delicate niobium necklace, from which hung a shark's tooth. That had been given to her the night before at the club by the men, in front of all their friends, during their collaring ceremony.

This was for the families, and the legal portion of the proceedings. "Families aren't just born, they're made," Loren said. "That's obvious by not just you three, but by most of us in this audience. We have families we were born into, and some of them accept us and some of them don't, but we've built families. Of both lovers and friends, of friends who became lovers, of friends who are so close they might as well be blood relations—Gilo, if you make a bloodletting joke, so help me, I'll smack you."

"Aww."

The audience laughed, and laughed again at the clueless looks on the parents' faces.

They couldn't help it. They were all well aware of how tragically close this day came to never being for a variety of reasons, and it felt good to laugh in celebration as well as victory.

When they were settled—again—Loren continued. "The bonds we make, the vows we take, the bread we break. It's all part of the tapestries we create together. And I feel blessed and honored to call you my friends. Kenny."

Kenny and Nolan flanked Betsy, all three of them holding hands. "Just because a piece of paper lists only one of you doesn't mean that we aren't a family together."

Ed Payne had made sure of that, the paperwork ready to file Monday morning, powers of attorney, a trust, and an LLC, in all three of their names.

He continued. "Nolan, we've been together for several years now—"

"How many?" Gilo called out.

"Almost seven, Gilo," he shot back with a grin. "Nice try. I heard Tony bet you."

"Dammit," Tony muttered from the other side of the audience. "I owe him twenty."

"Nolan, we've been together for nearly seven years now, and while it's been a wild and crazy ride, I wouldn't have ridden it with anyone but you."

Even Loren snickered.

He glanced at her. "Say it."

"Ridden. That's what *she* said."

The audience, already on the edge of hysteria, burst out laughing again.

And it was all expected by most. Betsy had made it loudly known that if people didn't cut up and keep the ceremony light-hearted and filled with laughter that she would sic June on them. Even their vows had been crafted with an ear to the ready one-liners.

"And I'm glad we have Betsy joining us on this ride," Kenny finished, smiling down at her. "Because I didn't know how much we needed her in our lives until she was there in the middle of it."

Loren snickered, which made Betsy laugh.

"I love you both," Kenny said. "And I'm glad I get to spend the rest of my life with you both."

Now it was Nolan's turn.

"I wanted to quote lines from *Rocky Horror* and *The Holy Grail*, and that got overruled for some reason, something-something-sacred, something-something-seriousness."

When that round of laughter died down, he continued. "You know, just to my left, is the man I had hoped to marry, and finally get to do just that. And then, just a step to my right, is the woman we both love and will cherish forever."

"I'm not putting my hands on my hips," Loren said.

"And it's too late for Leigh to keep her knees tight," Lucas said as he draped his arms around her and patted her baby belly.

That round of laughter took a little longer to settle down.

Nolan smiled down at Betsy. "I thought Kenny had made a monogamist out of me," he said. Then, in a mock British accent, he said, "But I got better."

Fortunately, Betsy had opted out of mascara and eyeliner, because tears of laughter were rolling down her cheeks.

"And boy, has it gotten better and better with you. I love both of you, and I know from here on out, things will only get better for the three of us."

* * * *

Betsy took a deep breath. So far, her men and her friends had far exceeded her expectations. "I don't know where I would be without you in my life," she said to them. "It's a hard idea to swallow—"

Competing rejoinders scrambled over each other. Someone called out, “That’s what she said,” while two others called out variations of “laden versus unladen” and “African swallow versus European swallow,” and someone even slipped in a “good girls swallow and bad girls spit.”

When it died down, she continued. “It’s a hard idea to swallow that I came so close to never being where I am today. Your love, your support, your patience—”

“Your pussy,” Loren playfully muttered low enough the audience couldn’t hear, but it cracked Betsy up.

“If it wasn’t for you both,” she said, “I wouldn’t have known the greatest happiness in my life, and I love you both so much.”

“Done?” Loren asked.

They smiled and nodded.

“By the power vested in me by the State of Florida, I pronounce these men husband and husband. And I pronounce these three a family of their own making. Start swapping spit.”

Kenny and Nolan kissed first, which was what Betsy had asked them to do.

Besides, it was only right her Sirs got to have the first snog as a married couple.

Then they each kissed her. And as the crowd erupted into applause, Loren leaned in to hug and congratulate them.

“Fess up, kiddo,” Loren said. “Which one of you deviants put my husband up to tossing the sex doll in the pool?”

It was fortunately floating face down in the water, but yes, one of the impromptu sex-toys-turned-pool floaty from the night of the baby shower-slash-kinky party had made a return appearance.

The three of them grinned at Loren. “We’ll never tell,” Betsy teased.

* * * *

It was a long, exhausting day. Someone managed to get the sex doll out of the pool before Nolan or Betsy's parents spotted it. By the time the three of them collapsed in the gulf-side hotel suite on Siesta Key later that evening, Betsy was hoping she'd still have the energy for a newlywed romp with her men.

She flopped onto the bed, still in her wedding dress. She'd been ordered to keep it on all day, the men loving the semi-formal strapless dress. She thought they looked pretty hot in their tuxes, too.

Kenny reached up under her dress, hooked his fingers around the waistband of her panties, and slid them down her legs. The only reason she'd been allowed panties at all was the very valid argument that she might end up so wet she'd get a spot on her dress and ruin it.

And the men certainly didn't want that.

She still wore her shoes as well, Kenny climbed up under her skirt and buried his face in her pussy while Nolan knelt by her head, unzipped his trousers, and fished his hard cock out for her to suck.

"Ravishing the bride," Nolan teased. "I like this game."

She did, too.

She smiled up at him, mouth wide and ready for his cock when he slid it between her lips. For the rest of the weekend, once her dress came off, she didn't get any other clothes until they were ready to give them to her.

And that was a condition she'd heartily agreed to.

She'd also enjoyed the fifteen cane marks they'd put across her ass the night before in front of their friends at the collaring.

There were a lot of things in her life she was able to enjoy again with them.

As Kenny's talented mouth and tongue worked on her clit, she sucked and licked Nolan's cock. He tangled his fingers in her hair and held her firmly in place as he started fucking her mouth.

"That's our good girl," he said. "Our very good, very beautiful slave," he said.

She stared up into his blue eyes. Yes, she was their slave. All of her. Down through the depths of her heart and soul.

They owned her.

And they knew it.

Even better, she knew it, and wanted it exactly this way.

It didn't take Kenny long at all to get her over. That was when he emerged from under her skirt.

"Change," he declared, rolling her onto her stomach and sliding her down to the end of the bed. Now her feet were on the floor, legs spread wide, the dress shoved up and Kenny's cock embedded deep in her pussy.

As she moaned in pleasure, Nolan returned his cock to her mouth. "There we go," he said. "Now you can make all the noise you want."

And she did. Every thrust Kenny took in her pussy shoved her onto Nolan's cock, and vice-versa. They seesawed her between them, building her up to another orgasm as Kenny used his fingers on her clit to get her over.

Perfection.

The world exploded around her, bright and clear, her men quickly catching up to her and filling her at both ends with their cum.

She happily rolled onto her back as they leaned in and deeply kissed her.

"Love you both," she said.

The men smiled. "Love you, too," they said in unison.

They'd talked about kids, but it wasn't a priority for her right now. She wanted to wait, to enjoy them, to enjoy being a family, the three of them.

She wanted to enjoy the right now.

Because it was all that was guaranteed, and she wanted to make the most of it, with the men she loved, who loved her. This carousel she now rode was beautiful, smoothly running, and even better, was perfect for them.

And it was a ride she hoped never stopped.

Chapter Twenty-Three

One year later...

June sat at the table and stared out at the water. It took her a while to finally speak. "Ross and Loren suggested I come talk to you," she said. "I was going to talk to Ross, since he's an attorney. But when he realized why I needed to talk to him he told me it was better if he didn't hear it. That's why I called you. To talk. Well, to listen while I talk."

The man across from her nodded but didn't speak.

She stirred her iced tea with her straw and took a sip before sitting back again.

"I can't even tell my husband this," she whispered, thankful that she hadn't worn makeup today that would run if she cried. "He thinks I'm up here visiting Clarisse today."

He still didn't speak.

She took a deep breath and let it out. "Maybe if I tell someone, then the nightmares will stop. It's been nearly a year and I still have nightmares. About how wrong it *could* have gone if I'd missed him, or if I'd hit her by accident. Or if he'd gotten closer to her with that knife. Thank god he didn't have a gun. But the nightmares aren't because of what I did. I don't regret what I did for a second. They're about what *might* have happened and didn't. Because I didn't just call the cops."

"You sound like it was planned."

"It kind of was. Not in advance. I came up with it on the spot. When I drove in to pick her up, I saw the car parked over to the side where I never saw one parked before on a weekend. Then I realized someone was in the car."

Sully leaned forward, his arms crossed in front of him on the table. "When did you realize it was Jack?"

"On the drive south. The car followed us out. I didn't tell Betsy about it. I thought at first it was a coincidence. Then I started driving a little slower, making sure I didn't lose him at lights, and I knew. There wasn't a lot of traffic that time on a Saturday morning."

She met Sully's grey gaze. "That's when I was sure it was that fucker."

"I thought you guys were supposed to go do what you did? Wasn't that planned?"

"Yeah, it was. But we were originally going to walk the trail there at Blind Pass Beach. She didn't know that. I let her think it was always going to be the other park, especially after."

He slowly nodded. "You baited him."

"I saw the fucker parked in the back part of the parking lot when we came off the beach after tai chi. I knew I'd have a better chance of getting a shot at him down south. Open area, more of a chance of it looking right."

Sully stared at her. "You really had been thinking a lot about killing him, hadn't you?"

"You were there that night. You helped rescue her. You saw her, what he'd done to her. What do you think?"

"I think Jack would have killed her, sooner or later, had she not left. That night was a test."

She nodded. "My sister was murdered by her boyfriend two months into our freshman year in college."

"I thought your sister ran a gymnastics school?"

"That's my older sister. My *other* sister was murdered." Her hand shook as she picked up the glass and took another sip of iced tea. "She was my twin. Nobody around here outside my family knows that but Mark. Scrye," she clarified.

Sully nodded. "So that's why you set Jack up, to give you a reasonable chance to shoot him."

"I was hoping for witnesses. I knew it wouldn't look right if he just jumped out and *bang* in the middle of woods. *Really*? I *just* happened to shoot the guy who attacked my friend, as if I was ready for him."

Sully smiled. "That's what happened."

"Yeah. But with a lot of witnesses. Thank god she was fighting, too. It drew more attention and allowed me time to get a good vantage."

"True. You okay for that?"

"Yeah. They cleared me. State declined to press a weapons charge against me considering I saved her life. First time I'm happy our state government is a bunch of gun-happy nuts. Finally got my damn gun back."

She took a deep breath. "I couldn't believe it, at first. I mean, he was supposed to be in jail. What the fuck was he doing *there*? I couldn't just go up to the window of his car and kill him sitting there."

"Security cameras?"

"Fuck, *yeah*, security cameras. At least three in that part of the complex. Damn Kel." Then, she laughed. "Geez, I sound horrible."

"I'm a writer, and a former cop," he said. "I do the same thing. It's a blessing and a curse."

Her smile faded. "It's why I never made the team," she said. "The US Olympic team. We were trying together. Yeah, we were a little older, but we were good. We were only seventeen. *So* fucking good. Then she died, and my heart died, too, that day. The grief killed my fucking parents. Slowly, but it did."

"What happened to the guy?"

She picked up her glass and took a long sip of iced tea before meeting his gaze again. "What guy?"

"The guy who killed your sister?"

She slowly shrugged. “That’s the pisser of it. He disappeared. He was listed as the prime suspect. Still is to this day, far as I know. No one was ever arrested for it, no prime suspect but him. Fucker had marks on his hands that looked like he’d beaten her, claw marks on his face, too, from her fingernails. She died with DNA under her nails that matched DNA from a hairbrush the cops found at his apartment.”

“How did they know he had those marks on him? I thought you said he disappeared?”

She looked out the window, at the murky water of the Anclote River flowing just outside the restaurant. “He did.”

THE END

WWW.TYMBERDALTON.COM
WWW.TYMBERDALTON.COM

ABOUT THE AUTHOR

Tymber Dalton lives in the Tampa Bay region of Florida with her husband (aka "The World's Best Husband™") and too many pets. Active in the BDSM lifestyle, the two-time EPIC winner is also the bestselling author of over eighty books, including *The Reluctant Dom*, *The Denim Dom*, *Cardinal's Rule*, the Suncoast Society series, the Love Slave for Two series, the Triple Trouble series, the Coffeeshop Coven series, the Good Will Ghost Hunting series, the Drunk Monkeys series, and many more.

She loves to hear from readers! Please feel free to drop by her website and sign up for updates to keep abreast of the latest news, views, snarkage, and releases.

www.tymberdalton.com
www.facebook.com/tymberdalton
www.facebook.com/groups/TymbersTrybe
www.twitter.com/TymberDalton

For all titles by Tymber Dalton, please visit
www.bookstrand.com/tymber-dalton

Siren Publishing, Inc.
www.SirenPublishing.com

CPSIA information can be obtained
at www.ICGtesting.com
Printed in the USA
LVOW01s1450250116
472165LV00018B/1497/P